The Nell Rescue

Andrew J. Van Auken

Thanks for all the support and friendship over many years. Always a pleasure and always will be!

Cheers!
Andrew Van Auken

Copyright © 2006 by Andrew J. Van Auken

All rights reserved. No part of this book shall be reproduced or transmitted in any form or by any means, electronic, mechanical, magnetic, photographic including photocopying, recording or by any information storage and retrieval system, without prior written permission of the publisher. No patent liability is assumed with respect to the use of the information contained herein. Although every precaution has been taken in the preparation of this book, the publisher and author assume no responsibility for errors or omissions. Neither is any liability assumed for damages resulting from the use of the information contained herein.

This is a work of fiction. Names, characters, places, and incidents either are the product of the author's imagination or are used fictitiously. Any resemblance to actual events or locales or persons, living or dead, is entirely coincidental.

ISBN 0-7414-3548-9

Published by:

INFI∞ITY
PUBLISHING.COM

1094 New DeHaven Street, Suite 100
West Conshohocken, PA 19428-2713
Info@buybooksontheweb.com
www.buybooksontheweb.com
Toll-free (877) BUY BOOK
Local Phone (610) 941-9999
Fax (610) 941-9959

Printed in the United States of America

Printed on Recycled Paper

Published November 2006

~ For my family and friends who gave me support.

~ For my wife who knows me best and has helped me at every step

Thank You

Cover Art by Randy L. Parker

Chapter 1

The year is 2005

It should have worked. After the move back from California, he had taken months to make that place a fortress where he could feel safe. The entry doors and windows had been fitted with discrete laser emitters in the jams. Tripping the silent alarm should have spread an array of lasers across all points of entry and exit, turning them into light powered meat slicers. Strobe lights, quietly located in every room would tell him if the grounds were violated, yet those hadn't been activated. The 'cable' hadn't been put into use, and frankly he was a little relieved. That security idea came to him in a dream and he quickly implemented it.

At a height of four feet in the two main rooms of the house, he had carefully laid a thin cable into the drywall by first making a slit with a utility knife and then covering it with joint compound. The cable ran under the drywall to a closet between the rooms where he had carefully threaded the cables together. It was then wound to a large pulley directly connected to a powerful electric motor.

Back in each room was a hidden switch that would activate the powerful motor and rip the cable from the wall, lethally separating everything in the room to a four-foot height. In the living room he had fashioned the switch to be one of the twenty buttons on the remote that no one ever uses, and in the large den it was a simple switch on the bottom of the desk. If someone ever got in he always thought he could get to the floor before hitting either of the panic buttons to avoid the fate of his intruders. Ever since the day he finished the installation he was always scared of dropping the remote or having the dog get under the desk. Little chance it would have of catching him anyways, he was mostly below the windows when inside the house.

And the dog, how could he forget the dog! He noticed his memory was a little fuzzy and suddenly couldn't recall what he had done that morning. The last he knew, the dog was sprawled out on the carpet of the living room. That was the dog's favorite spot and it was a comforting feeling to see him so peaceful. He was a young Rotti with big feet and sharp hearing, the perfect defense. His big feet webbed out in the soft dirt around the house and would give anyone the impression of a full size watchdog. His hearing sometimes picked up the shutting of nearby car doors, which put both of them in a panic, but it was worth it. The sight of that dark eyed angered dog always gave him back the feeling of control. That dog was just about the lowest tech system in the house and yet it seemed to give him the most comfort.

"What is his name? I'm looking right at him, what the hell is his name?" he whispered in the dark.

"Something's wrong," he said. He did seem to remember misplacing things the day before. First his new shirt he had bought and never even wore. And then the hat his brother let him wear. His brother Jake was going to be pissed, that was his favorite hat and wore it all the time. And how does someone loose a toothbrush? Every night like clockwork, Gable brushed his teeth, and always tossed the toothbrush back in a cup by the sink. Now as he moved forward in his head, a complete blank awaited him for the morning's events.

"I must be going crazy," he thought to himself. "It's the paranoia finally catching up with me." None of that really mattered now. Now it was cold and dark. He felt the steel all around him and his claustrophobia and nervousness started to take hold. It felt like he'd been buried alive, no air to breathe, no light to define his surroundings. He frantically felt the floor for signs of a seam or anything recognizable as being man-made.

His eyes were wide now, ready to accept any scrap of light, but there was none coming to them. The sounds of his movements gave him the feeling of a large room.

"It must be at least 20 feet across in here," he said to himself. As he slowly crawled forward on the metal floor, he held his arm out for fear of colliding with a ledge or a wall in the dark. Reaching a wall, he felt something familiar. It was a bead of weld, which he followed upward with his fingers. He knew what weld felt like and that it was probably made by human hands. This seemed to calm his breathing slightly.

Many questions began racing through his head. How did he get to this place? What was this container he was in? Who brought him here? Why him? The 'Why' question he knew for sure.

That was about the only thing he knew for sure.

Chapter 2

One year earlier

Gable Flagstaff was a middle-aged industrial engineer living and working in California. A few years prior he had moved from Buffalo, New York where his closest living relative still lived, his brother Jake. Gable was highly successful but rarely had time to savor the spoils. Friends had told him about these hiking trips up in the mountains and one day he thought, 'how bad could that be?' Fresh air and a little exercise, perfect for getting him out of the office for a while. His brother back east said he should fly back for a little vacation, but he decided to travel to Yosemite Park instead to have a new adventure. This decision would prove to be one to change his life forever.

The journey started out normal enough. Gable was big on research and had read a lot of hiking magazines during the weeks before his hike. He meticulously packed his gear the night before the drive out to the camp. He broke the handle off his toothbrush to save space and chuckled at the thought it would really make a difference, some tip he read in a magazine. He was having fun focusing on something other than work so it didn't matter anyways. A new pack with an external aluminum framework sprawled on the bed. He had bought everything new when he realized nothing in the closet was going to work for this trip. A new sleeping bag, whistle, enough socks to fill a drawer, even a compass and Swiss army knife. The brochure said to bring eating utensils too, so he had found a bag of sporks. He tossed it on the bed, smiling at the consolidation of utensils. The next day he would drive two hours to the lodge shown on the brochure, to meet up with a guide and hit the hills. He was second-guessing the directions already.

It only took a few direction-giving gas stations to get him there, but he arrived at the lodge early in the morning on a beautiful warm day. There was a scattered group of ten or twelve people droning around the small parking lot apparently looking for some sort of direction. He pulled his gear out of the back seat of the car and headed for the sweeping deck on the front of the building where most people seemed to be migrating to. Gable felt more comfortable off to himself as he waited for the small groups to form. The director promptly came out of the great hall inside to greet everyone and welcome them to the hike.

"I want to thank you all for coming out this weekend for what looks to be marvelous weather for hiking! You will all be divided into two groups today and paired up with one of our very experienced Trail Guides." Just then, as if on cue, two young looking fellows stepped out to join him.

"I'd like to introduce Shaun and Gary, two of our park's most knowledgeable guides. They will help you to organize and be on your way. Thank you again for hiking with us." The director quickly shuffled back into the building as the guides went to work discovering who was with who and how many people had turned out for the trip. Gable fell into a group of four other people, two sisters traveling together and a father and son. Their trail guide was a 22 year-old college kid who looked like he had been doing this gig every summer since he could walk. He gathered them all together off to the side and introduced himself.

"Gather around people, my name is Gary. Looks like a good turnout today. We're in luck for the hike, the weather reports all say clear. This is a beginner to moderate skill level hike for the weekend so I'm sure we'll all have a lot of fun. We'll leave here this afternoon and hike down to Lower Jackass Lake where we will make base camp. Saturday, you will have a choice of swimming, fishing or some lower level hiking. For anyone who feels up to it that day, there are some moderate hiking trails up to the high passes of Madera Peak. On our third day we'll be hiking back to this lodge. Any questions?" The small group stood silent either embarrassed to speak or waiting for their next direction.

"Great, let's go inside, get everyone registered, and check our gear." With that the energetic guide turned and pushed open the doors of the lodge. As they all entered the large hall they could see multiple tables set up, each one had a sheet of paper on it with a list.

"Everyone grab a table please. You'll find a list of all the things that you are going to need for the trip. If you've forgotten any of these items, please let me know and we can provide them for you. I'll help you repack and then we'll group up for some brunch before hitting the trail." Gable walked up and heaved his pack onto the first table. He pretty much had everything on the list except for a few small items; he had taken a long time to prepare. Gary walked up to check on him.

"How we doing today?" asked the guide.

"Good, good. What's this bandanna on the list for?" he asked

"Well, you can use it as a wash cloth, sweat band, tourniquet, a number of things." Very nonchalantly Gary started to unzip the main compartment on Gable's rig. Towels and socks swelled out of the opening. A small smile slid across Gary's face,

"You'll want to be packing as light as you can for your first trip down the trail." He looked quickly at the sticker on Gable's shirt. They had all been branded with nametags when they stepped in the lodge. "Here Gable, let's exchange these three washcloths and this towel for this bandanna," he quickly pulled a red hankie from behind him, "and get rid of half these socks. There are plastic bags for 'return to car' items at the ends of the tables. Don't worry, happens to everyone first time out. What else you got in this truck?" he said jokingly as he poked the sides.

"I'll take a look," Gable said as Gary nodded and headed off to another hiker's pile of equipment. Other tables now had the contents of hiking packs strewn across them. The two sisters obviously had a beauty pageant in the schedule judging from the amount of cosmetics they had. Gary was actually helping them pack plastic bags with the stuff himself. The father-son team seemed the most prepared; the son was giving directions as if he was an Eagle Scout. Gable reached into a side pocket on his pack and moved about a small video recorder until it faced out at him; he didn't dare take it out. He found the power and record buttons and made a quick recording.

"Well, here we are, first day of the hike. We've got the Power Puff Girls and the Scouts of America on this trip, I'm in trouble already." He quickly shut it down and closed the pocket as Gary approached.

"When we get going today I'll be your hiking buddy, ok? We had one person cancel from the group but we always pair up. That sound cool, Gable?"

"Sounds fine, great," he said as he stuffed the recorder deeper into the pack. After brunch and some mild stretching, they headed down the path. The first night was uneventful; campfires, stories, marshmallows. All you'd ever expect. The next day Gable felt like more of a challenge and decided to hit the Peak. It was late afternoon before he convinced Gary that he could handle the uphill hike and they both set off. Gary was able to actually hike and talk at the same time, further proof that he was in much better shape than all of them.

"Ok, Gable, here's the plan. I'm going to get you up in here and let you find a place to sack for the night. I'll have to head back down and make sure the rest of our group eats dinner. I'll be back up in the morning, does that sound all right?" They were only an hour and a half up into the hills and Gable was wearing down already, but he tried to hide his lack of breath with short answers.

"Sure," he answered. Gary had seen it before and chuckled under his breath. They pressed on further until they began to enter the high passes of Madera Peak. "This is fine, right here," Gable said.

"Ok, partner, it'll be getting dark in a few hours so I'm going to hustle back to camp. You have everything you need?" Gable looked around the area and gave Gary a nod.

"Great, I'll see you in the morning then," said the guide. "Be careful now. We'll see you," he said as he headed off. The darkness was coming quick and Gable decided he should get going to prepare. He scavenged about for bits of dry pine twigs and vegetation that he could use for his night's fire. He made a little pit, just as he had seen Gary do the night before and assembled his kindling in a pyramid. Going through his pack, he searched for dry matches.

"Crap!" he exclaimed. He just then remembered giving them to those girls last night so they could light candles in their tent. He was angry with himself now but there was nothing he could do. Dusk was well on its way and there was no time to get down to the camp so he decided to at least find a spot with some better scenery for the night. He muttered the curse one more time aloud as he threw his gear on his back and headed up the hill.

He found a perfect place to set up for the night. It was a high ridge above one of the mountain passes. There was just enough light left for him to roll out his sleeping mat and get his bag set up on it. He stirred in his new North Face sleeping bag as the darkness overtook the ridge.

"Ok, too damn hot!" He was constantly reminded that he might have gone a little overboard with indulgence for the trip. The terrain across the ridge was undisturbed; nothing was out there, no lights, no noise, just peace. Far in the distance he slowly noticed lights coming through the valleys of the rolling hills. They were at least two miles out and traveling single file.

"That figures," he thought, "who the hell is this gonna be? Probably some kids looking for a good time away from Silicon Valley. Jeeps, gotta be Jeeps." The headlights were high, off-road vehicles for sure, but the lights were spread far apart.

"Huh, definitely Silicon Valley; rich kids in Hummers." He hoped they'd get lost or just break down somewhere so he could watch them unravel out in the wilderness. At least it would be a perfect chance to try out his night vision video camera he had purchased for the trip.

That thing broke all the rules of hiking. It was heavy, and was truly just a luxury, but he loved the chance to try out technology. The monstrous vehicles were under a mile from him now. He saw they would eventually pass through a low point of the hills hundreds of yards below him. There was no way they were getting through there, an obvious obstruction was in their path, although the dim night made it impossible to make out. Didn't matter, they'd have to stop there and he could check them out with the camera.

The video camera was in his hiking pack next to him and he adjusted around to find it again in the side pocket. Rummaging around in the pack he also came across a granola bar that had shifted around during the hike.

"Great, popcorn for the show," he thought, and rolled back over on his side to face the excitement. The vehicles were still coming, slower now, laboriously climbing through the rough terrain of rocks and pines. 'Granola was a good choice,' he thought. Light to carry, good energy, and it couldn't melt in the heat! He tossed the wrapper on the ground next to him and threw the bar in his mouth. He was eating it like a cigar as he fumbled to get the camera on. The light in the eyepiece put off a light green glow. As he put the rubber eye boot to his face, the granola bar slipped from his mouth and hit the dirt!

The opposite hill across the valley was alive! The steep hillside across and below him had at least a dozen people crawling on it. There were two groups of people staggered separately about 200 yards horizontally apart. He activated the zoom. It was enough to see that they were lightly armed and dressed in dark clothes.

"What the hell!" he whispered. He was up on his knees now and had gotten himself out of the sleeping bag without even knowing it. He spun to the group of Hummers. Their lights dimmed the night vision slightly and it took a minute to re-adjust. With the zoom still active, he could now see that the people inside weren't kids at all! They were dressed in camouflage military fatigues. He could see clearly the sweeping antennas stretching from bumper to bumper on the trucks, and the large top-mounted weapons confirmed these were military. He suddenly felt very exposed kneeling on the ledge. His hands started to shake as that nervous panic feeling started to hit him. This was partly the reason he needed this vacation, as these panic attacks had been happening too often. Even out here he couldn't escape it!

He quickly went to his belly and took his eye away from the camera. The calm view of the landscape returned to merely kids in Jeeps driving through the hills. The darkness easily masked the activity in the shallow gorge. Now lying as flat as he could, he brought himself back to the camera eyepiece. The green glow was inviting but Gable was nervous at what else he'd discover. The men on the hill face were gone! He could hear the engines now lightly echoing up from the valley. As he panned down to view the noise, he caught the men's movement. They were fanned out now and seemed to be converging with the military vehicles. They all seemed to be heading towards the large mass blocking the path in the low spot of the road. He reset the zoom now to capture the vehicles and the spot that hid the men all in a single frame.

Suddenly the lead vehicle stopped as the other two took positions on either side of it. Light bars that he hadn't noticed before, quickly crackled to life and illuminated the area ahead.

It was an unreal scene, one that Gable would never forget. A craft shaped like a large flat teardrop sat dormant in the pass ahead. It lay on its belly with the large lobe of the craft facing the vehicles. It was as long as a mobile home and as wide as two of those Hummers. The rubble around the craft looked freshly disturbed, this thing obviously had touched down a short time ago. It was hard to tell if more of the craft was below the surface

"What the hell is this?!" he whispered to himself. His arm was killing him, but he couldn't put the video camera down. He watched on, constantly reminding himself to breathe. For what seemed endless, all parties were at a standstill. Gable was frozen on the ridge, the darkly dressed teams on the hill seemed to be dug in with their weapons up, the men in the Hummers sat confident behind their bright lights, and the ship lay inactive at the center of it all.

Then very quietly a figure began to materialize on the backside of the ship. It was humanoid looking, and stood a big six-foot at least. The physic did not appear overly muscular, but more toned and built for speed. Details and close features were lost at the distance from the ridge; even the zoom of the new camera couldn't bring it close. He could however distinguish rough outlines of the creature's face. It appeared dark and hollow. Where its eyes and upper section of the nose should be, only a single horizontal dark oval spanned across its face. Another such shape stretched vertically down the remainder of the face area, centered below the eye. This feature was more sunk in and shallow. The legs of the beast were long and jointed like a man's, as well as its arms. Its neck seemed to flow into the shoulders very smoothly giving it an aerodynamic sort of look. The skin of the creature appeared stretched as if its body had grown too fast.

The creature had emerged silently and seemingly undetected. It was on Gable's side of the ship and obscured from the sortie of men on the opposite hill. It slowly knelt down and doubled over till its head came close to the ground. A light groan came from deep in the beast and ended with a loud shout that wasn't like a shout at all, more like a loud grunt! The noise shattered the silence and visibly startled the men hiding on the hill. From their position they couldn't pinpoint the source of the noise and they quickly formed two back-to-back huddled masses in the darkness. He tried not to lose focus of the creature, but the scream from the beast had his hands shaking again. His eye was sore from staring at the scene through his little green window and he could feel his pulse pushing against the eye boot of the camera.

The creature was then silent. It stayed in that lowered position for only a few seconds and then its motion seemed to explode. It stood up quickly, but translucently away from its body as if its soul had stepped away from its frame! The erect figure seemed just as solid as the first, and it was easily discernable. It moved to the rear of the craft, staying low and out of sight of the men. The second creature had removed itself from the valley floor and now seemed poised to come in exactly Gable's direction!

Quickly the center of the ship began to emit a light glow. What took only three to four seconds, the glow seemed to vibrate and flash like a small shimmering strobe. The two creatures seemed slightly more visible now as Gable believed the soldiers on the hill caught their first glimpse of what was moving around the back of the ship. The closest group, still three hundred yards from the ship, began to maneuver defensively. The being closer to Gable's direction shot into a sprint, heading away from the ship and towards the smaller plant life and pine trees far below him.

His first few steps seemed blurry, as if you were watching it move through the bottom of a glass. Gable swore the entire creature then became blurry and then completely disappeared yards before entering the small pines! The other creature had sprung over the back of the spacecraft and was now suddenly on the far side facing up at the men. The shimmering light from inside the craft quickly sped up now, throwing the tall creature's eerie vibrating shadow onto the hills. The ship put off a low hum for only a moment, and then all hell broke loose.

The creature flinched forward and at that time the ship fell silent with one large burst of light. It took with it all the electrical energy in the area! The lights of the Hummers all went dead, and an electrical shock jolted the video camera from Gable's hands. He fell backwards into his gear as a quiet blackness filled the valley below.

For a second there were only the sounds of his camera crashing down the steep bank into the dark abyss. The pounding of his heart was choking, and he could feel it trying to leap from his chest. The camera came to a rest, or at least something had stopped its fall. BOOM! An explosion of concussion grenades and automatic weapons fire rose from the pass. Gable retreated back to his North Face sleeping bag, curled in a ball and held his ears. The noise was incredible!

"IT'S OVER HERE, OVER HERE!!!!!" The shouts from the soldiers where panicked and mixed with the weapons fire. "IT'S RIGHT H........." Something had cut the shout mid-sentence. And then a loud explosion! The firefight settled for a few seconds. Dead quiet. Gable seemed to begin his breathing again and squinted his eyes to look around him. He broke from his fetal position and started a low crawl back towards the ledge. He could smell smoke and could see a fiery glow from the crest. He was ten feet away now, dragging himself as close to the ground as he could. Suddenly the shouts came to him again!

"THERE! GOING UP!!!! GOING UP!!!!" Chunks of dirt began to fly from the ridge where Gable was hiding. Small rocks and grass landed all around him. He could picture those guns on the trucks firing away, and indeed they were. Down in the small valley there were far fewer soldiers involved in the gun battle now. The able men were focusing their fire back up towards Gable's ridge. Two of the hummers were getting a cartridge bath from the .50 cals mounted atop. The operators were blinded in the dark by the muzzle flashes and were wildly scattering their fire across the face of the steep hill. Gable stayed low but continued to look forward across the few feet to the ridge. The edge was exploding and crumbling away from the bullets' impacts.

Suddenly a strange arm reached over the edge and stretched half the distance to where Gable lay silent. Startled by the sight, he squirmed backward like a snake in the dirt. The noise of the guns and shouts became faint as a sloped dome grew over the edge from where the arm came. The shape formed into a head, as it seemed to be trying to escape from the firefight. Everything seemed quiet now to Gable and in slow motion. The smell of the smoke was clear in his nostrils and he could see the growing glow of flames in the background. The alien shape was crisp now and only a few feet away. Dirt silently exploded all around the figure as it tried to pull itself over the edge. A large bullet tore through its shoulder as it sharply turned its head away. A second shot caught the turning head square and destroyed the features immediately. The carcass of the creature turned instantly lifeless and slipped back over the edge.

Sounds came rushing back to Gable as if he was emerging from water. There were a few more shots, the engines of the HumV's, the crackling of a large out of control fire, and at the top of it all, the pounding of his heart. He gripped his hand in a fist and cursed his nervous shaking.

He noticed he was covered in something wet, the creature's remains he assumed. It was clear like water with only a hint of viscosity. There was very little scattered material from the alien around for what had just happened. He should have been covered.

From the edge he could hear the men and the trucks moving around. The fire was quickly getting out of control and he knew he had seen enough. Gable frantically shoved everything into his pack that he could find, but it seemed like there was more room now.

"The camera," he cursed himself. "Can't worry about it, gotta move!" He was sure he had everything else. As he threw the pack on his shoulders, he heard a new sound coming from far behind him. Down the pass that had brought the other vehicles now raced a large covered truck coming towards the scene.

"I'm outta here," he said as he hastily made his way back down the trail. He was tripping and stumbling in the dark but at least he was getting away. More than he could say for that creature.

Chapter 3

His hands now continued to explore the wall of the chamber. He felt an arced piece of steel and bolt heads in a circle. Metallic sounds now. A circle of light appeared from the center of the circle close to his hands. His pupils quickly shrunk as he stepped back startled. The new light gave him the first look at his long and tubular container. The floor was plate steel spanning the shape, giving it a flat surface to stand upon.

The light dimmed as a human face appeared behind the glass of the view hole. With a nod from the man, more mechanical sounds, and a small round door opened at the end of the chamber throwing light all around.

"Mr. Flagstaff, if you'd be so kind to step forward." A man in a white lab coat motioned for Gable to move toward the door. Behind the man Gable could make out other similarly dressed people sitting at laptops and viewing large flat screen displays.

"Where am I?" Gable shouted, "Who are you people?!" His voice echoed out of the chamber. He felt like a mouse in a cage, trapped and forced to do what his owner wished.

"Please, Mr. Flagstaff, all your questions will be answered if you'd just step out and allow our technicians a few moments." He backed away from the doorway clasping his hands in front of him.

"You are near Cassel, California at a facility owned by SETI. You currently stand in a decompression chamber and have just had an experience that demands a short medical examination and I would very much appreciate your cooperation," the man in the lab coat said immediately. He then stood silent, away from the door.

"Ok, fine," Gable muttered as he reluctantly moved toward the light; muscles tensed. He uncomfortably took the doorway with white knuckles and peered out into the room. The room wasn't very large, but it was full of very expensive and sophisticated equipment. There were six people that he could see, most sitting at computer equipment and not obviously disrupted by his presence. The walls in the distance seemed curved to him, like it was a round room. His examination of the room was abruptly cut short.

"Please sir, have a seat here." A technician pulled forward a chair and motioned for him to be seated. As he did, the technician and another examiner began to take simple vital signs.

"Your name is 'Gable' Flagstaff, is it not?" The man who had first spoken was now asking the question. After accepting a positive nod from Gable he replied, "Very good, very good indeed. My name is Doctor Edward Richards. You have been brought here to assist your government, thank you very much." He turned as if he was going to exit quickly, and walked to a nearby table.

"Hold it!" Gable was persisting against the men taking his blood pressure and touching him with their cold stethoscopes.

"Why am I here and why me?!" He was putting his questions directly to Dr. Richards' back. The doctor looked over his shoulder and quickly retorted,

"I think we both know the answers, Mr. Flagstaff." He turned his back and negotiated around the table in front of him. Gable caught a glimpse of the table. On it was a plexiglass case; inside sat a charred video recorder!

A prick on the arm. Quick look.

"What was th…" Gable slipped into the dark.

Chapter 4

Dr. Edward Richards wasn't actually a medical doctor at all. He was more of a student of the paranormal and the powers of the mind. An interest he never thought would pay off until he was contacted by SETI years ago. SETI (Search for Extra Terrestrial Intelligence) has a small shadow branch that handles its research and development and is funded directly from hidden funds in the government. This R&D group has limited military and technical resources available to it and is not affected by funding cuts put on SETI itself.

The doctor exited the Chamber Room into a large elevator, which took him one level down. As he entered this second area it was obvious that he was in charge of this facility. Lab personnel and computer techs in the room all greeted him with 'Hello Sir' or a respective nod. This room was exactly the same size as the one above it. The edges of the room met with curved walls but it was more apparent here for lack of computer equipment. Rather in the center of this room there resided a large rectangular tank supported horizontally at waist level. Hoses and wires spewed from its sides and ran down across the floor and up the walls to the room above. Two men with small hand held computer pads stood next to the tank as Dr. Richards approached.

"How did it hold up," asked the doctor as he put his hands on the corners of the container. The tank was long like a coffin and fully sealed. All its walls were made of stainless steel and only a small two-foot square piece of tempered glass inlayed into the top allowed visibility inside. That window now lay at the end below the eyes of the doctor.

"Worse than the last transport sir," replied the attendant. "I don't know how many more we can pull from him before we lose him."

"We will sustain 'it' for as long as possible. Keep your fingers crossed, it took us 10 years to get this far and we are barely unlocking its secrets. Now that we have the right guy, maybe we'll be able to keep this program going. Hopefully he saw something before Recovery went to shit last year. If we don't have something of value here then we'll all be out of a job. We need to get that craft open, and I fear that this decade old creature may be the only key." His eyes panned down through the glass at the large oval eye of the face below. Inside lay a creature artificially alive submersed in a thick amniotic fluid. Tubes entered its body as wires and electrical feeds exited the back and top of its head.

Chapter 5

Hours later, the effects of Gable's injection were wearing off. He found himself in a small room on a rough military style cot. The room had no other furnishings, only the cot and a single door with a slim vertical offset window. He could see the reinforcement in the glass and it reminded him of an institution. He sat up on the cot and held his groggy head with both hands.

"A short medical exam, huh. These must be the military guys from that night. Damn that recorder," he muttered as he pounded a fist on his knee. He stood and moved to the door. He immediately confirmed it was locked with a jiggle of the stainless handle. From the window, he could see across the narrow hallway outside. Two similar doors with narrow windows stood on the opposite wall. As his eyes focused, he peered into the furthest room's window and noticed something familiar on the end of the cot inside.

"What the hell is that," he softly spoke, "That's Jake's hat! How'd that get here." From his angle Gable could only see the end of the cot and on the brown military blanket sat his brother's cap!

Now with both hands banging on the door, he started yelling wildly while remaining focused on the other room. Then a foot lazily extended onto the end of the cot and came to rest next to the hat. Gable could see no more of the room than what the small window allowed, but what he did just see silenced him immediately.

Just then, a large man dressed in military fatigues filled Gable's window and motioned him to step away from the door. As he complied, the door opened inward and the military figure stepped into the room. The size of the man seemed to almost fill the tiny cell. Behind him came Dr. Richards pulling a rolling office chair.

"Please have a seat Mr. Flagstaff. No harm will come to you, you have my assurance," he said as he seated himself in the chair. "I will try to answer some, I'm sure, very pressing questions you may have." Gable nervously seated himself on the cot, keeping his eye on the large soldier.

"Firstly, I would like to apologize for our processing methods. Your course of action over the past months has made this strategy necessary. You've been very busy keeping yourself unavailable. I promise you that what I have to offer is a chance to help your country. You undoubtedly realize that we are all connected to a certain incident a year ago near Yosemite. What you witnessed was unfortunately a complete disaster orchestrated by our military resources." Dr. Richards shot a glare back at the officer who seemed to deflect it with a stern look of his own.

"Operation Recovery was supposed to be a simple task. We had detected the landing of a foreign craft two days prior and organized a small team to investigate. Captain Mitchell was in charge of the team," now facing the officer, "Would you like to give a short brief of the 'operation', Captain." He had a sarcastic tone in his voice as he gave the floor to the Captain.

"Based on intelligence provided," he looked down at the doctor with a cold glance, "two ground teams were sent in to investigate the sight. Upon arriving on location we were attacked by one of the creatures. It was unfortunate that it had to be destroyed." The Captain related his account very calmly with arms crossed.

"Destroyed?! You destroyed the whole damn valley!" Gable started shifting on the cot as though he was going to take some action.

"You damn near killed me when it got close," he said in a low angry voice. Dr. Richards then interrupted,

"That is precisely why you are here, Mr. Flagstaff. Contrary to my colleague's thoughts, I believe you may have seen something that I desperately need to confirm. Captain Mitchell reports he engaged with two separate creatures, one of which seemed to move completely undetected through the vegetation," he explained as he leaned forward in his chair.

"It was a master of camouflage or my men would have had a chance to properly do their job," added the Captain.

"Camouflage, hell, that thing went invisible, I saw it," Gable interrupted.

"Exactly, Mr. Flagstaff, that is my belief also! It is also my theory that this pair of creatures was in fact produced from a single entity. This creature has the ability to force itself thru a mitosis process that equally divides and recreates itself. Its mind is incredibly powerful and can control its own cell structure, an ability that unquestionably helps it survive in the vacuum of space. Some on my team think that this level of control can somehow be used to align its molecular structure and produce an invisibility effect. Now, you also never saw the creature actually 'exit' the craft, did you Mr. Flagstaff?" The doctor seemed excited like a boy at Christmas as he continued to quiz Gable.

"You seem to know a lot about these things already, what do you need me for?"

"Unfortunately, upon demise of these creatures, their physical remains seem to quickly disintegrate into the air. There is a theory that without the mind to hold the body together, it rapidly disperses. I need to confirm that these creatures carried on these traits and for lack of physical evidence, I can not."

"Then how do you know they can do these things at all?" Gable asked back. A long sigh came from the doctor. He looked down to his side and seemed to now sit uneasy in his chair. Gable continued, "and who is that in the other room?!"

"I must apologize again, but we are not fully to blame. We've accidentally brought your brother here." The doctor said plainly. Gable stood immediately and the Captain quickly drew a yellow Tazer weapon from its holster. Their eyes met briefly and Gable returned his glare directly at the still seated Dr. Richards.

"He is in excellent health and really does not know where he is anyways. You see, he has been sedated ever since we discovered he was not you. So please, sit down and let's continue," he said nonchalantly. Gable was angry and started to feel that tense sensation come over him. His hands balled into fists at his side and he began to lean into a step towards the man. Suddenly the loud clicking of the Tazer weapon could be heard filling the room.

"Just sit down buddy, or you'll be laying down." Captain Mitchell had the weapon squarely level to Gable's chest with his finger on the trigger. Looking down he saw a bright red laser dot unwavering on his upper body. He grudgingly returned to his seat and listened as Dr. Richards laid out his amazing story.

Chapter 6

"In mid-1993, I was contacted by SETI to consult on a new project. This 'new project' was born of a crash landing of a craft not unlike the one you witnessed. This ship impacted Madera Peak in southern Yosemite Park and came to rest in the high passes of the area. At the time we were highly funded by NASA and had an abundance of ground scanning satellites available to us. A thirty-minute window of visibility existed and a Landsat satellite started recording. What it recorded was amazing, Mr. Flagstaff." The doctor continued.

"The hull of the ship was completely ruptured and this could easily be seen from the footage. A being clearly materialized away from the wreckage; a creature similar I believe to the ones destroyed a year ago. In the recording it was obvious that the creature was injured from the crash. Although unclear, it then seemed as though the thing replicated itself and became two distinct individuals. After the event, the injuries and effects of the crash appeared to increase. One of the pair instantly fell to the ground and began to disintegrate. This is when we discovered the unfortunate consequence of their death here on our planet. The other one stumbled around the site for quite some time, it too also seemed greatly weakened." Gable was captivated by the story but was also concerned about himself and his brother's safety. With that soldier around he knew there was nothing he could do.

"Mr. Flagstaff," the doctor continued, trying to keep the attention of his audience, "this creature then made himself invisible to the satellite and was gone. SETI, of course, immediately dispatched a containment crew to control the situation. This creature was found unconscious and again visible a few hundred yards away from the site. It was taken into confinement and brought back here."

"You mean you've seen these things before?" asked Gable.

"Yes, but one more point of interest remains," he said, brushing off the question. "Before the team arrived, a completely unclothed human stepped forth from the wreckage. He was observed stumbling away from the wreck but the satellite never got a definitive glimpse at him. They searched for hours to find him, but turned up nothing. With the one crash victim and daylight approaching, they needed to wrap up the scene. It was assumed he was probably an abductee that caught a lucky break during the crash. They've never been able to track that person down, but more importantly they had one of the creatures; and that's where I came in."

"In September of 1993, NASA dropped all SETI funding. The project had to be moved to the R&D Group so that we could continue funding thru back door money from Washington. I became Director of that operation. Since that crash we've been trying to discover how to harness the power of the creature. You see, like any good business you must turn a profit. SETI projects are constantly on the chopping block for government spending, and our funds are not far from running out themselves. We need to show the government that we have benefit and those abilities are exactly what the military would be interested in. Imagine, Mr. Flagstaff, the ability to transport a soldier instantaneously over vast distances, and once there to replicate that soldier before engagement. Now imagine this battalion of soldiers could become invisible to the enemy!" Dr. Richards could barely hold his enthusiasm as he unfolded every detail.

"So this thing is still alive?" Gable asked

"Indeed it is. In fact, its capabilities are exactly what brought you here; your brother first for that matter. Since acquiring the alien, we've only been able to tap its teleportation abilities. By connecting powerful circuitry to its brain, we are able to control this function although I'll admit currently there are some kinks in the system. We have found it quite unchallenging to transport inanimate objects, although without physical DNA it is impossible for us to move live specimens. When we finally tracked you down, we needed to acquire you without making a scene. You've been under surveillance for a week now awaiting an opportunity, but unfortunately we had a bit of a schedule crunch; teleportation became the ideal way to seek your audience. Since the only object of yours we had was your camera and its broken bits of footage, we needed to quietly attain a DNA sample. A new and fresh sample is required for each transport, and if we know the exact location of the subject, well, the experience is instantaneous."

"DNA sample?" Gable shot back with a contorted look.

"Yes," Dr. Richards answered, slightly annoyed by the interruption, "a hair or saliva sample is best. We first teleported a shirt from your home, that you were witnessed purchasing, in hopes of a sample, but it came up clean. After our initial failure, we took a ball cap that you were seen wearing. Imagine our surprise when we opened the chamber to find not you, but your sibling. The results of our final operation brought you to us now. So you see, it's partially your actions that have involved him thus far."

"So what's with the chamber?" asked Gable.

"I can see now, Mr. Flagstaff, that I've captured your interest," the doctor said while he eased back in his chair.

"I just want to know what's going to happen to us now that you've put us through that thing!"

"The procedure is well documented at this time and poses no long term threats. We have found through early testing that when our computers control a transport, the test subject has to be brought directly into a high-pressure atmosphere. If not, the subjects would suffer from what you commonly know as 'the bends'. You should be thanking us that you weren't one of the first one hundred sheep through the gate." He looked to the side and exchanged a childish grin with the Captain. Gable was not amused.

"Other than short term memory loss upon arrival, all is normal. You assuredly felt some disorientation when you appeared. So, you see, you will be entirely fine. The problem is the military's not interested in a fighting force that immediately forgets what their mission is. They need assurance we can continue our research to fix this problem and it seems the creature aquired years ago is soon to expire. Operation Recovery was to renew this program and give us a fresh start. Now from that operation I am left with only a beautiful ship that we can't open and no physical evidence that it was even the same creatures. I need to open this new ship and hope that maybe we'll find another clue."

"This is all great for you, Doc, but what's it gotta do with me?" Gable said somewhat defiantly.

Dr. Richards smiled slightly at the refutation and leaned forward placing his arms on his knees. He took a deep breath and then continued,

"Mr. Flagstaff, in two days I will be meeting with some very important sponsors on the topic of funding for this facility. I will need that meeting to include conclusive evidence that the recent acquisition of the alien craft will further my research in teleportation. The craft is seamless with no apparent functioning hatch. You alone have seen that this species of creature is capable of transporting himself outside the craft without the use of doors. I will expect a recorded affidavit from you tomorrow of the events at the site. This is simply all we need from you." The doctor relaxed in the chair outwardly exhausted from the explanation.

"That's it? That's what all this is about? If I do that, we're free to go?" Gable said with a puzzled look on his face. He couldn't believe that all the trouble he'd gone through over the past year, all the worrying and preparation, all of it had been for nothing.

"Of course I'll help, and then my brother and I can go, right?"

"We'll book the flight at the end of the interview," Richards said smiling. "Of course for your own safety, we'll need to monitor you tonight in this room for any unusual effects of the transport. I assure you all is fine and this is just standard. You'll see your brother in the morning after the taping and you both will be on your way by the afternoon." He stood from the chair obviously pleased with the meeting and turned towards the door.

"You guys got a bathroom here?" Gable quickly shot.

"Of course, Mr. Flagstaff, my apologies. Captain Mitchell, would you be so kind to show our guest the facilities?" directing his attention back to Gable, "Dinner will be served in your room in just a little while. We are not usually with company so I'm sorry for the inconvenience. I'll see you in the morning, Mr. Flagstaff" He stepped through the door into the hallway.

"Gable. Call me Gable"

"Of course, Gable. Thank you again for your cooperation. Captain." The doctor nodded to the soldier and then exited down the narrow hall and around the corner. Gable felt very much relieved and safe as he stepped into the hallway and followed the soldier. As they passed the room where he had seen the hat, he abruptly stopped.

"Hey, where did Jake go?" He looked at all angles through the glass window, as if it would give him a better view of the tiny room.

"They must have taken him upstairs for a few routine tests. Nothing to worry about I'm sure. The restrooms are right down here." The Captain motioned for him to go to the end of the corridor. "I'll wait here." He leaned against the wall with his legs and arms crossed

"Ok, you do that." Gable continued to the end of the hall. The bathroom was even smaller than the room he was being held in. It was as though these facilities had been an afterthought of the building. The outside wall of the bathroom was curved, similar to what he'd seen in the Chamber Room. After taking care of business and washing his hands in the small sink, he exited the bathroom back to the hallway. As he approached his waiting escort he thought he'd try to get some more answers.

"So, Captain Mitchell, what is this place anyways?" He didn't really expect a reply but he thought it was worth a shot. Surprisingly the Captain provided conversation as they walked back down the hall.

"You are in, what appears from the outside as, a controls silo for the BIMA Millimeter Array. We're smack in the middle of Hat Creek Radio Observatory high on a dry plain in California. Sounds romantic, don't it. Topside it's just a bunch of radio dishes and dust, not much to look at. This level is about two down from the surface. Don't worry, you won't be here long." The speech ended back at the small cell. "Here's your stop." Captain Mitchell ushered him in and closed the self-locking door. The mechanics made a definite lock.

"Ok, this won't be too awful I guess. A little dinner, stupid tape thing in the morning, and then we're outta here. Ok," he said as he settled back on the cot. Gable seemed to be trying to convince himself that everything was going to be ok, and it almost would have worked.

"They tell you lies." A strange ghostly voice loudly filled Gable's head as he nearly jumped off the blanket!

Chapter 7

The BIMA Millimeter Array is a system of 10 moveable dish antennas, each roughly 15 feet tall and 20 ft in diameter. They can be driven and arranged on the ground in different patterns to achieve different observations of signals from space.

But the latest activity at the Radio Observatory is the new Allen Telescope Array. This project is being run jointly between the University of California at Berkeley and SETI itself. When complete it will be a field of 350 radio dishes, each roughly twenty feet in diameter, capable of receiving signals from space deeper than ever before. It gets its name from Neil Allen, the founder of SpaceTech and also the person who personally donated 26 million dollars towards the project. His young company's contributions to Radio Astronomy have helped to pave the way for deep space exploration. The ATA Project was solely a SETI project and could provide no funding towards the ever-separating branch directed by Dr. Edward Richards. Mr. Allen visited often to check on progress but because of information firewalls between programs, he knew nothing of the activities in the silo.

Dr. Richards had left the lower level where he now had Gable captive and took the stairs up to the first sub level. This appeared to be more of an office area for the personnel of the disguised structure. A few doors from the stairs sat his office. It was a medium sized office decorated mostly with shelves of scientific books and miniature models of experimental aircraft and other trinkets. The executive desk paired a tall plush chair that was backed against the one interior silo wall. Dr. Richards came swiftly through the wide heavy door and moved immediately to his chair. In a tray near the corner of his desk lay an earpiece and mic. He put the device into his ear out of habit and logged into the computer at the desk, bringing the large flat screen monitor to life. Fifteen minutes or so passed before an electronic voice message sharply relayed to the earpiece.

" * Incoming Message * "

"Accept." Dr. Richards' keyword opened up a video connection on the screen before him. He was looking at a professionally dressed female assistant sitting in a large wooden paneled office.

"Dr. Richards, will you hold one minute while I connect you to Senator Brandt?"

"Yes, of course," he answered to the woman. The open screen went to a simple color scheme as he waited for the connection.

"Ed," the voice came to the earpiece as soon as the link was made, "How are things?"

"Everything is going well, Senator. Thank you for your call. What can I do for you this evening?" The doctor looked into the screen at the Senator who sat in his own office, grasping what looked to be a half full brandy glass. Shadows of movement and distant glances from the Senator gave the impression there were other people in the room. The time difference made this a late-night call from Washington, which made the doctor visibly nervous.

"In 48 hours we will be flying across this country and a few of us are nervous that this will be a waste. I must be honest that I feel the same way. I do not need to remind you the delicate funding channels feeding this project. A lot is riding on a successful return, Doctor." The Senator sipped his brandy uneasily.

"I can assure you that we've made direct links between Operation Recovery and the '93 Crash. I believe the presentation will be convincing enough to persuade you to further fund the research, Senator. You see, we are very very close."

"I haven't 'seen' anything yet. I need to put on our man's platform that he can reform the military and it's operations in order to win the public vote. They're not moving election dates as far as I know!" he said as his face grew in the video window.

"No sir, they're not. You'll be pleased when you get here, Senator. You have my guarantee." Dr. Richards tried not to look away from the web cam but he could see that Captain Mitchell was now silently standing in the doorway of his office.

"Two days, Doctor. We will see you then." The Senator reached forward and the picture was gone. Richards eased back into his chair and tossed the earpiece into the tray. He spoke through his hands as he rubbed his face,

"Tell me only good news, Captain Mitchell," he said.

"The first one's on the plane, smooth sailing. The other one's down there wining. My Private said that something your delivery boy said set him off and now he wants to see you." The Captain was leaning against the doorway with his arms crossed.

"Does he realize it is eleven o'clock in the evening," the Doctor said as his hands dropped to his lap.

"If you remember, I said to increase the dose so we wouldn't have to deal with him at all until the morning. This is already getting too sloppy," said the Captain.

"Ah yes, so we could spend all of the next day explaining to him what happened to him hours ago and that he'd been drugged ever since his arrival. What then, Captain, a written statement read while under gunpoint off camera. No sir, I don't think that's the sort of thing we need here. The gentleman needs to be comfortable, calm and convincing. I will humor his request and see what the hell he wants. After the taping, we'll never have to deal with him again." Dr. Richards lifted himself from his chair and crossed the office laboriously.

He squeezed past the man in the doorway and stepped out into the hall. Once past the door the Captain asked with a sarcastic tone,

"You need help down there?" The Doctor paused for a moment and looked back at the man in military clothes standing smugly in his office door.

"I'll page you if I need you. I don't plan on taking long." He pushed opened the stairwell door and headed down to the lower level.

Chapter 8

Gable looked around, frantically searching for the source of the voice. He could see nothing; only the cot and he occupied the room. Frozen on the cot, he tried to think if the voice was out loud or just in his head. The door lock suddenly released and a man in a lab coat quietly entered the room with a covered tray.

"Sir, Dr. Richards sends dinner for you." Out in the hall stood a military escort that was keeping a close eye on the room.

"What was the announcement for?" Gable asked the server.

"What announcement do you mean?"

"The announcement just now. The public address system? Wasn't there an announcement?" he asked, lightly grabbing the arm of the man.

"I didn't hear anything." The man sat the tray down on the edge of the cot and backed away from his grip. He was a little disturbed by Gable's comments. "It's just a few sandwiches and chips. It's not very often we have a guest here."

"You mean 'guests', right?" said Gable

"Leave the tray, let's go," scuffed the Private in the hall. The man stepped back through the door and turned into the corridor. As the soldier reached in for the door handle, Gable snapped at him.

"Tell Richards I want to see him!"

"Sure buddy, I'll get right on that for ya'." The door made its resounding lock sound as Gable stepped up to the tiny window. He could see the soldier walking out of view, but he realized for the first time that he could not hear the footsteps. Soundproofed rooms; that's why his brother couldn't hear him across the hall. That made sense to him, but there were also no speakers in his room. He chalked the voice up to exhaustion and probable side effects from the transport.

"When I get out of here tomorrow, I'm gonna sue the crap out of this place!" By now it was late in the evening and he hadn't eaten since midday. Lifting the lid on the tray he got a look at the main course of the night. The peanut butter and jelly sandwiches looked like they had come from someone's uneaten bagged lunch. In the few minutes it took to devour the meal, he decided it really didn't matter. He was also pretty sure that Dr. Richards wasn't going to be coming back tonight. He started to feel again that he was more of a prisoner than a guest.

"It will all be straightened out in the morning," he thought, "and then we'll get the hell out of here." Sliding the tray on the floor with his foot, he lay back on the cot to try to get some sleep. He no sooner shut his eyes,

"*You'll never leave this place, Gable.*"

His eyes opened wide. It was the same voice and tone as before, and he now thought it had to be inside his head. Still writing it off as an ill side effect, he closed his eyes and lay still with his head resting in his interlaced fingers.

"I'm ignoring this," he said quietly.

"*That would be a mistake,*" said the voice. Gable remained silent.

"*I can help.*" The voice was persistent but the tone was still very calm and steady. Gable was busy trying to figure out how much psychological damage would be worth in a lawsuit. He was also thinking that it must be a coincidence that the man bringing the food did not know about Jake being there too. Someone else probably brought him something to eat, he thought.

"*Your brother is far from here, Gable*"

"I wish this would stop," he whispered as he squeezed his eyes shut.

"*You are not in control of it. You need to realize this.*"

"And why is that," he muttered mockingly.

"*For I can help,*" said the voice calmly again. Gable chuckled slightly. If he was going crazy, he thought he might as well play along for a bit.

"Help what, help us get out of here?" he questioned back to the voice.

"*I can help 'you', the other has been removed.*"

"What's going on here? What's happening? Where's Jake?!" Gable sat up trying to find something to direct his conversation to. If this was real then what was the source of the voice? Who was talking to him?

"*They have given your brother a drug that will eventually wipe his memory of all he has experienced here. I have seen it before during the earlier tests, when they transported the humans in tattered clothes. It causes the human to slip into a coma like state for at least two of your days. They have him on a plane now and will leave him a few thousand miles from here. They'll make it look as though he was in an accident and all will be covered up.*"

He swung his feet to the floor and pushed his palms into his eyes. "That doesn't make any sense. How do you know that?"

"*After your testimony tomorrow, you are to be detained here indefinitely for study. They believe that you had contact with the Braxton at the landing and through a series of tests you will help provide the answers they seek. Gable, after tomorrow morning, you will never see home and you will never be awake again."* The inner voice gave all the information very bluntly. It continued,

"I need your help and in return I can save you from this fate."

Gable had tried to stop the voice in mid-sentence but could not. Its owner was not he nor controlled by him. This was really happening, but he still didn't know who was communicating with him.

"How do you know these things? Who are you?" he asked back.

"I need your help to find a man. All I know is that he is alive. I will answer your questions, but I must first know I have your help."

"Can you take me to my brother?" asked Gable.

"There is nothing you can do for him, he will be cared for at a hospital and released upon expiration of the drug."

Gable thought for a moment about all he'd been told. Dr. Richards had said he'd go free, but why would he ever let him go? Why would he ever do that, he thought.

"I've seen the inside of this place and he explained the whole plot to me. Damn, he was never gonna let me go. That makes sense about Jake; at least he'll be all right in a few days. This is some sick dream!" Gable thought silently to himself.

"You are correct on almost all points, Gable," said the voice immediately after his thoughts concluded.

"You can read my thoughts too? Should have assumed that. Fine, I'll help you however I can, just get me outta here." He was standing now talking as if he was at a podium, slowly looking side to side as the words came out of his mouth.

"That's great news. Do you have a safe place you can think of that you'd want to be?" The locking mechanism on the door started to deactivate. Someone was coming in.

"Yes, I can think of one," he said hastily. The door began to swing inward.

"Picture it now, Gable, in your mind's eye." The door half opened now. Something gripped his arm.

Dr. Richards stepped through the door to the vacant room to find nothing there except for the cot and an empty food tray! Slamming the door open into the wall, he pushed back into the hall and ran towards the stairs grabbing at his pockets for his pager.

Chapter 9

As if he had blinked, he was standing in his own home, he could tell by the way the light entered through the blinds in the room. Something still held his arm, he could feel the heat and pressure, but then quickly it was gone.

"Are you still there?" Gable said aloud.

"*I am here. This is your home?*"

"Home sweet home. This is amazing! We were just in California, and now Buffalo?! Where are you?" He looked across the room, scanning the light that the street lamps could push through the blinds and drapes of the room. "You're one of those creatures aren't you?"

"*What you witnessed was a Braxton. They are our warrior class and one always accompanies a space voyage for security. I was there at the landing one earth year ago but stayed within the craft when they destroyed the Braxton. I tried to assist the battle by using the ship's energy disruption capabilities, but I could not stop your kind. I have been in hiding since that time, searching the facility for clues and spending time dormant in the ship.*"

"Dr. Richards said that he couldn't get inside the ship. So you *are* teleporting in and out, just like he thought." Gable was comfortable now as he felt his way towards the couch and slumped into the cushions. Still speaking out into the empty room and answering the voice in his head, he continued. "You said 'searching for clues', clues to what?" Gable slumped further into his couch as he waited for the response.

"*Clues to help me find the man,*" said the voice.

"Right...right." It was now very early in the morning according to Gable's internal clock and the exhaustion was catching up with him. He'd woke up on a metal plate and a flat military cot already today, and the comfortable end pillows of the couch swiftly pulled him into a deep sleep

Back at the Observatory, Captain Mitchell's pager vibrated off the small nightstand and hit the floor. It had been a long day already and he was in no mood for one of Dr. Richards' little emergencies. Reaching down from the bed, his knuckles scrapped the floor searching for the noisy device. Without opening his eyes, he grabbed it as it began making its way under his bed. No sooner did he touch the backlight to see the number on the display did Dr. Richards burst through the door.

"He's gone! Tell me you've moved him!!" he screamed at the groggy Captain.

"Why the hell would I move him? What do you mean he's 'gone'?" asked Captain Mitchell as he sat up in his bed.

"Gone, Captain, as in the man is not there!" The doctor turned and bolted back out of the room assuming the Captain would be close behind.

"This guy could screw up falling out of a boat," he said as he swung his feet out from under the sheet. With no real sense of urgency, he dressed from the pile of clothes that he had taken off only minutes ago and headed out of the room. When he reached the bottom of the stairs of the lower level, he could see Dr. Richards standing down the hall in front of the small room. As he approached the empty room Richards repeated his findings,

"Gone, just like I said." He held out an arm into the room as if the soldier wasn't going to be able to see the emptiness that was left.

"Well, were did he go?" he said as he peeked his head around the side of the doorway. The doctor, not amused by the sarcasm, moved close to the soldier and spoke roughly.

"Find him now and make sure he doesn't leave again. He cannot be allowed to ruin this operation!" He stormed past the man as the Captain turned and said,

"Hey, it's almost morning!"

"Well then, I suggest your men find him quickly!" the doctor said as he rounded the foot of the stairway and headed up. The next few hours found men scouring the high plains in search of the escapee. Hummers broke the area into a grid pattern with foot soldiers filling the gaps. At the facility, scientists and lab technicians tore the place apart, room-by-room. Dr. Richards stirred in his office, listening to the commotion outside his door. A hand held radio on the corner of his desk crackled away with dismal reports from the grounds outside.

"Sir, we've covered out twice as far as he could have gotten. He's not out here," came a voice from the radio. Dr. Richards dropped his head into his hands and let out a deep breath. He reached for the radio and hit the transmit button.

"Bring them back, Captain. Lock this place down; we will resume the search internally in the morning. Let's be fresh tomorrow, we must find him!" He dropped the radio on its side and eased back into his chair, rubbing his eyes. He was tired also and could almost fall asleep in his chair. Next to his office he had converted a small conference room into a makeshift sleeping quarters where he spent most his nights. He was unmarried and often worked late, so he stayed at the building. Pushing himself away from the desk, he moved towards the other room and rolled onto the bed, quickly falling asleep.

Morning at Gable's house seemed to come quickly. He slowly opened his eyes and looked about the now bright room; there was a noise in the house. He lie still momentarily, trying to decipher the footsteps. From around the corner came a jubilant black dog, stumbling around the furniture and coming straight for his face. Gable quickly sat up as the dog got one good lick across his face.

"Ughhh," he muttered as he wiped his face and pushed the dog away. Seeing the dog and the familiar surroundings was rapidly reversing his memory loss.

"Ok, Taz, ok, down boy. You want to go out, I bet you do." As he lifted himself from the couch and headed for the door, he wondered if it had all been a dream. He no longer heard the voice; maybe it was a dream, a bad dream. After letting the dog outside he took a quick shower to refresh himself followed by a short inspection of his house. He strangely did not feel alone although the house was completely empty.

"Hello, are you still there?" he said to the empty room.

"*Yes, I am here. They search for you now at the facility,*" said the voice.

"Well, thanks to you I don't have to worry about it." He walked to the kitchen, as he spoke to himself, and pulled down a cereal box. He glanced up at a clock showing 10:00.

"So, I guess that all happened, huh." Gable seemed at ease this morning and well rested as he carried on his conversation. Pouring out his cereal he asked further, "So what are you? Invisible right now or just a voice in my head, what's the deal?"

"*I can appear completely invisible to your human eye in this oxygen rich environment. If we were on my planet in our much thinner atmosphere, I would not be so transparent. An advantage of your planet that I'll continue to use for both our sakes.*" Gable crunched away on his breakfast and listened to the words in his head.

"*My species communicates telepathically as our atmosphere greatly hinders the transmission of sound waves. I understand this is probably an uncomfortable experience for you.*"

"It takes some getting used to. So how about the teleporting, all of you do that too?"

"*Each of my kind is born with the ability to transmit themselves great distances, it is just part of our genetic make up. Upon adulthood, the ability to displace one's cellular structure begins to develop. On Earth, you witness this as invisibility. If nurtured, it can become an easy feat to control.*" Gable walked to the sink and added to the stack of dishes before heading into the den. He walked and talked trying to further understand the creature.

"So why did you come here?" he asked.

"*Many of your Earth years ago, an explorer craft intercepted a probe from your planet. It contained information on your species and the galactic location of your solar system. It was taken back to our planet 12 billion light years away in the Ultra Deep Field and examined by our Higher Clergy. Deciding that you were not ready for contact, your planet was placed under observation. In your year of 1990, we witnessed your placement of a space-based telescope at an orbit of 375 miles from your planet's surface. You would recognize it as Hubble. We interpreted its capabilities and decided it might be able to detect our planet, and this chance could not be taken. A Cleric volunteered for the mission to immobilize the threat and began the journey to your planet.*

Through enhancement circuitry on our spacecraft, we are able to use our minds to push space travel at incredible speeds by teleporting maximum distances controlled by the ships. Even at maximum velocity, it took him until your Earth year 1993 to reach the space telescope. We detected that he was a success when you launched the first of many service missions later that year. The degree of sabotage was planned to be severe enough that you would never be able to recover the capabilities again. Although his assignment was complete, he never returned from your solar system.

I was sent here to investigate the incident and recover the Cleric. Scouring your planet from space, our systems were able to determine where he came down to the surface. We were there only 24 of your hours before they attacked my craft."

"And that's what I saw last year?" Gable asked.

"*Correct.*"

"So what's this Braxton you mentioned before and who is this Cleric guy?" he further asked as he began logging onto his computer at the desk.

"*The Higher Clergy is comprised of our top scientist and religious figures. The scientific disciplines of the Higher Clergy have been experimenting with the Braxton for quite some time. They used to be very much like us but we kept their race enslaved. Through breeding and chemical alteration, the Clergy have brought their race to a whole new level and added powers that make them ideal for aggression.*"

Gable paused for a moment, "The replication," he said as he looked blankly to the side.

"*Correct again. When they replicate, their strength is temporarily divided for a few moments until cell activity rises to full capacity. They are typically very efficient in the effort.*

Meanwhile the religious faction of the Clergy has conducted their own research into our powers of body and mind. A short time ago they were able to perfect the conscious control of their genetic makeup itself. Through mind control they were able to change the outward appearance of themselves and transform into other species of our planet with comparable mass. Since the discovery of your probe, they have taken on your human form and have even begun to mimic your language, although audible speech is nearly impossible in our thin atmosphere. Also their duration in humanoid form has caused most of them to lose their invisibility capabilities"

"So what are you saying, that you're walking around on your planet looking like us?"

"Only some religious leaders experimented with the ability. They behave fanatically at times and often believe they will bring eternal peace and enlightenment to our people, appearing to the population as if some greater power had touched them and transformed their bodies. Most commoners know nothing of the discovery of your planet and the threat that the Clergy see from it. To the Higher Clergy, it is imperative that I return with the Cleric. It was announced that his journey was a Mecca, one of illumination and enlightenment for our people. If he does not return there is fear of a loss of faith in the Clergy, and they cannot afford this to happen."

"So the 'man' Dr. Richards spoke of from the crash, he's really one of you?"

"I need to find this Cleric, return to my ship, and bring him home."

Chapter 10

Across the street, two men worked slowly packing up surveillance gear and eating breakfast burritos. The listening device that had been directing a laser at the window across the street had been dismantled and packed the day before. Feed back from the laser had allowed the vibration of the glass from sound waves inside the house to be decoded into words and conversation. The large camera and telescopic lens now lay tucked inside a padded hard case resting on the bed. The two agents were happy to be done with this boring stakeout assignment and were already planning where to get their second cup of coffee on the way to the airport.

"Hey, the guy's dog got out," one agent said as he poked his finger through the blinds. Back across the street indeed there was a dog out. Taz, Gable's black rottweiler was sniffing around the front bushes oblivious to the men.

"Probably got a dog-door somewhere. Forget about it, we're outta here. Hand me that tripod." He continued to pack equipment: phone tapping devices, video recorders, and high-end laptops. He shut his laptop, slid it into the carrying case, and tossing it on the bed behind him. His partner backed away from the blinds and went to the kitchen of the house, where he had his own laptop set up. It was still running an energy-tracking program on the house across the street, which tracked usage spikes at the power box. It was sensitive enough to pick up a nightlight. On the screen was a traveling line much like a heart rate monitor, showing a steady pattern of highs. They determined it was the refrigerator operating automatically. The screen had held that pattern ever since the day before, when the California team had abducted Gable. He reached to close the laptop when he noticed the indicator line was at a slightly higher level!

"That's strange," he thought as he traveled back to the window and peeked between the blinds again.

"What now? Let it go," said the other agent sitting on the corner of the bed.

"Shut up, would ya! Get that laptop back out and give me the surveillance shots of that house!" Reluctantly the man slipped the computer back out of its large carrying case.

"Ok, give me a minute," he said as he sat the computer on his lap and waited for it to boot up. As the last of the boot up programs ended, he already had the cursor over a folder on the desktop labeled 'Flagstaff.' A few double clicks and he was staring at a gallery of photos of all angles of Gable's house. "What do you want to see?" he asked.

The first man moved away from the windows and got behind the laptop, now showing a slideshow of digital pictures.

"Show me doors, man, just the doors." He watched intently as the screen showed him all the exits of the house. His hand quickly reached inside his sport jacket pocket and pulled out a thin cell phone. He clumsily flipped it open and gave it a single voice command, "Mitchell!"

Captain Mitchell was still in a deep sleep when the call hit his cell phone. It was still only after seven in the morning in California, but given the situation, he had overslept anyways. Inside the facility the personnel had already begun searching for Gable. Rolling out of bed he searched the floor for the source of the chirping and found it after lightly stepping on his pants a few times. He quickly pulled it out; convinced he was going to miss the call.

"Captain Mitchell," he sleepily said into the phone. The voice quickly came back,

"Sir, it's Douglas and Adams, in Buffalo. We were packing."

"You should be on your way back now, what's the problem," he cut him off.

"Yes sir, we're closing up shop now. We may have a problem, sir, we have activity in the house." The agent was quick to his point as to not get cut off again.

"What kind of activity?" The Captain was quickly getting dressed now and moving about the room.

"There's been a breach at a door of the house, Flagstaff's house, and I've got a power spike from inside. Nothing got by us sir." There was a pause on the line as the Captain thought it through. Douglas and Adams were experienced field agents and if they thought something was going on, chances were it was. He needed answers before briefing Dr. Richards so he decided to authorize them to check it out.

Inside the house Gable shut down the computer.

"Well, I thought we could just search for your guy on the web, but I guess that's out." He spun in the chair now facing the open room. He thought back, remembering what the Braxton looked like, and it fostered a question, "So friend, what do you look like?"

Outside the house Taz lay tranquilized by the shrubs as the two agents split up going down each side of the house. Agent Douglas was at the den window now with his back to the house. He peered up into a small round mirror that he held on a telescoping wand. He could see through a part in the blinds that Gable was sitting alone in the room with his back to the window. He reached down for his phone again and immediately contacted the Captain.

"Sir, he's inside!"

"Who? Flagstaff? That's impossible! Authorization is given to enter and detain. Report when complete!" The connection to California went dead as Douglas activated the 2-way radio function on the cell phone.

"Adams, do you read?"

"I'm here, I'm down from the front door," Adams answered.

"Flagstaff is inside in the room farthest from your location. I am by the window entrance. We are authorized to enter and detain. He's alone, come through the residence and I'll cover from the window."

"Roger that. Piece of cake. I'll be at the door in ten seconds." Adams worked his way down the side of the house crawling behind the shrubs and below the windows. Just before reaching the door, he failed to notice a series of small bare wires protruding horizontally out from the house. They were roughly six inches long and at least a dozen of them stuck out in a line. Unaware of their existence, he brushed through them and reached the door, but as the bare wires touched, low voltage current jumped between them and completed the circuit.

Inside the den, Gable awaited an answer to his question. Quietly the red strobe above the window began to turn, alerting him of the silent alarm. Outside, Douglas witnessed the change in behavior in the target but was oblivious to the silent light rotating above the window. At the front door, the embedded devices had finished warming up the internal lasers and now threw a field of horizontal lines across the entry. Adams was now out from the bushes and standing at the door. He tried the knob first; still unlocked.

"Piece of cake," he repeated. He pulled a .40 cal Glock 27 from inside his jacket and forcefully pushed through the door. The agent may have had a chance if he was not tight to the door. He would have seen the quick smoldering and almost instantaneous burn through of the door at each laser location. Instead, the agent barely made a sound as the wooden door provided no shield and the laser system that Gable had installed worked flawlessly. Gable quickly removed himself from the chair and bolted out of the room. The entry way was full of smoke from burning pieces of the door and the severed pieces of the agent lay all about the floor. The sight made him sick.

Outside the window Douglas was unsuccessful at reaching Adams on his radio. He quickly stood up and looked into the room. Strange strands of red light spanned across the inside of the window.

"Tricky bastard," he muttered as he pried the window open. He was careful not to touch the field of lasers as he reached for a collapsible knife he always carried in his pocket. Quickly swinging out the knife he pried into the jam and wiggled the long vertical receiver on the right side of the window. He knew if he misaligned the sending and receiving units, the laser system would fail in the window. As soon as the misalignment was enough to defeat the system, he quickly jumped up into the window and slid onto the desk that was positioned tight to the wall. Gable heard the noise behind him and darted back to the den. At the doorway he could see the man with a leg still in the window scrambling across the big desk. It felt like it was slow motion as he sprinted into the room and dove to the floor in front of the desk. He twisted to his back under the piece of furniture, searching for the hidden switch he'd installed. The agent was now flat on his stomach on top of the desk and reaching down towards Gable. Gable's hand was at the switch, but he paused.

"Where's the alien? Oh God," he instantly thought. The agent now had Gable's shirt and was yelling wildly. Gable looked down past his chin to see his shirt being crumpled by the man's fist and could see out into the entryway a pool of blood creeping across the linoleum.

"Now or never," he thought as he closed his eyes and flipped the switch.

The sound of the relay on the electric motor in the closet was loud and clear. The fast motor whirred to life as it quickly wrapped the cable into its pulley.

The thin cable broke free from the drywall and whipped across the room and in an instant Gable saw pictures and pieces of drywall board flying everywhere like he was in a war zone. From under the desk he heard a short yell as the man's grip swiftly released. The motor in the closet quickly stalled out and shut itself down.

He slowly pulled himself out from under the desk and surveyed the room. It looked as if a tornado had come through! Glass from picture frames and open books littered the floor; the drywall dust was almost choking. In the corner lay the agent crumpled up with his feet in the air. He was alive and seemingly uninjured. Gable found him to be unconscious and missing only a shoe.

"Must have caught his foot," he thought. "You're lucky buddy," he said aloud to the slumped agent and then turned back towards the room. He never got a chance to warn his unseen friend about the device and now was concerned for his safety. Searching around the debris and waving off the dust he again heard its voice,

"*I am still here, Gable,*" it spoke clearly in his head.

"Oh jeez, thank God. I forgot to tell you about that," Gable said apologetically.

"*I must thank you for your pause before activation then. In those moments, I was able to see the device in operation through your thoughts and teleported myself out of this room, saving me from it.*"

"Do you have a name, friend?" he asked.

"We do not have names, only mental impressions. In your language our Clerics have given our race a name. We are called Nell."

"Ok, I guess that'll work. May I call you Nell?" After a pause, the alien voice responded,

"As I am here representing the security of my kind, it would be an honor to be named Nell. Thank you," the voice said.

"'Nell' it is then." Gable knelt down to check the pulse of the unconscious man. He reached inside the agent's jacket and removed the Glock from the underarm holster.

"He won't be needing this," he said as he flung the weapon out the open window. "We can't stay here Nell, more will come here, I know it."

"Then where?" Still in his thoughts was his brother. It was at that moment he felt Nell touch his shoulder; and they were gone.

A few minutes later Agent Douglas slowly came to. He dragged himself flat onto the floor and searched his pockets for his phone. He coughed in the dusty room and looked about at the destruction. His ankle was throbbing and the pain was almost unbearable as he placed a call to Captain Mitchell.

"Captain Mitchell," the phone announced.

"Sir," grunting from the pain, "we lost him, he's gone."

"You idiots! How did this happen?" the Captain shot back.

"He was ready for us, sir. Sir, Adams is dead and I'm badly hurt. We need an ambulance in here," he pleaded.

"Then you better make that your next call!" The Captain slapped the cell phone shut and slammed it on the desk in front of him.

Chapter 11

Gable suddenly found himself standing in a room staring through a large window at an Intensive Care Room. A nurse walking by noticed him standing in the dimly lit room looking through the glass.

"Excuse me sir, you can't be in here. Visiting hours don't begin until one o'clock for ICU," she said respectfully.

"I know ma'am, I'm family. What happened here?" he asked her.

"Relation and name sir?" she replied. Gable continued to stare through the glass at Jake lying on the bed.

"I'm his brother. My name is Gable, Gable Flagstaff." She was still writing the information on her multicolored clipboard when she spoke again.

"The doctor would like to speak to you if that's all right." Gable couldn't pull his eyes away from the patient lying peacefully in the next room.

"Yeah, sure, I'll talk to him." With that the nurse disappeared.

"*We should not have come here.*" Nell's voice was still monotone and clear in his head.

"I know what you said, but I couldn't help worrying about him, he is my brother," he said out loud. From behind him came a quiet voice,

"Of course you couldn't." A doctor offered his hand, "Hello, my name is Dr. Hartsmon. I'm the doctor on call today. You say you're the patient's brother? Your brother had no form of identification on him when he was brought in. There are some forms I'm going to need you to fill out if you don't mind. What is his name?"

"Jake. How did you say this happened, doc?"

"Well, your brother is very lucky to be alive. He was actually found unconscious on the side of the road. The police believe it was a hit-and-run, but there are no blunt impact wounds of any sort on his body. He is in a coma now, but breathing completely on his own. This is a good sign, but we still cannot predict when he will wake from it. I'm sorry," he said as he placed his hand on Gable's shoulder. They both stood facing the glass as thoughts of guilt plagued Gable's mind. He couldn't help to think that he dragged Jake into this.

"By the way, how did you know that he was here?" the doctor questioned.

"A friend told me he saw him come in. Doctor, could I have a minute alone please if you don't mind?"

"Of course. I'll be outside," he said exiting the room.

"I want to destroy Richards, Nell," he whispered angrily.

"When I find the Cleric and leave in my ship, that will destroy him. The captured Braxton is soon to die, and after its passing, he will have nothing. We need to find the Cleric now, Gable," Nell said. Gable stepped away from the window and sat down in the nearest lounge chair.

"How do you propose we find him?" he asked as he settled into the chair. Letting his head rest back on the chair cushion, he rubbed his eyes as he listened to the voice in his head.

"After spending time on this planet, I realize that your species needs three things to survive: food, clothing, and shelter. For him to stay in human form for 12 years and assimilate, he must also have these things."

"Money, Nell, he'd need money." Gable sat forward in the chair as he spoke. "Where's an alien running around looking like a naked guy gonna get money?" Gable thought for a moment about what jobs the Cleric could have taken on and where someone without skills could readily be employed. He was kind of proud of himself for thinking like a detective, and then the voice hit him with the simple solution,

"Wouldn't he just take it?" Nell had said earlier that all of his kind are born with the ability to physically transport themselves. The Cleric could of easily used that ability here to get money and other items. 'Why couldn't he just zap himself into a vault and clean it out,' he thought. Nell picked up his thoughts and answered the question.

"We can only transport to a place we can see or have seen before or is a thought or memory of another. Wouldn't this make it difficult?"

"Maybe, but at least it's a start. Nell, take us back to the sight of your landing a year ago." In a flash Gable was standing on a ridge overlooking a small valley full of new scrub growth and rotting remains of timber devastated by fire. Gable stepped up to the ridge and collected his thoughts.

"They tried to blame the fire on me last year; the Captain was good at covering his tracks. Luckily, without matches, they had a hard time proving that I could start *any* fire. I guess for once it was good not to be prepared. So this was also the site of your friend's crash?"

"All of our research confirmed it," the voice replied.

"So not knowing any place here on Earth, he had to walk out, right? We need maps. Let's go, we've got some hiking to do back to the main lodge." Gable sighed as he remembered the trek up to this point a year ago. At least it was only after nine in the morning in the park and the sun wasn't high in the sky yet. He turned and began to hike down the overgrown trail as he thought about the area maps he had seen in the Great Hall during registration.

"Excuse me, can I help you?" said the man as he rounded a table and walked across the large room towards Gable. Gable glanced to the side to see him coming and then looked forward again. He was standing in the Great Hall in front of a map encased behind a piece of plexiglass on the wall.

"You could at least warn me before you do that," he whispered. Turning towards the man, he now recognized him as the director of the lodge, he replied, "No thank you, I'm just looking."

"Hey I recognize you. Have you hiked with us before? Sure you have, you were with the group that got tied up with the fire business last year. We're all very lucky there was a crew of smoke jumpers near our area at the time; they did an excellent job containing the fire. I apologize again for placing blame, you understand it's rare that we ever have an incident here at all," blurted the director.

"No harm, no foul. Only you can prevent forest fires, right?" he said jokingly trying to break the awkwardness. "I'm actually just checking the hiking map here for a friend. He wants to sign up for a hike but he's worried that he might get lost. If someone were to get lost in this area here at the passes, where do you think he should go?" he said pointing at the map.

"Where a person should go and where he does go are often two different things when lost in the wilderness. If the person has a compass, then he should head due west towards this lodge and the closest main road. But a person lost and confused in the woods will tend to travel in the path of least resistance, mainly downhill. If your friend were to get lost there," he said putting his finger on the plexiglass, "the terrain would probably take him south and out of the park somewhere near the town of North Fork. Tell him not to worry about it though; we have very experienced Trail Guides here that will help organize and plan a perfect hiking experience." Gable had to cut him off before the director put on his salesman hat.

"Well, thanks," he said as he began to step away. "I just wanted to get the info for my friend, I guess I'm all set for today."

"We run hiking tours every day, we'd be happy to set something up for him. You have a good day now," the director said as he turned and headed back across the hall. Gable briskly exited the hall onto the large front deck facing the parking lot.

"Don't suppose you can transport my car here can you," he joked. "I've got an idea, but I'll need your help," he spoke softly as he looked out onto the lot of cars. Opening the door into the hall again, he spotted the director sitting at a tall counter across the room.

"Hey buddy, I think your lights are on out here," he shouted across the room.

"Really, damn, let me look," he yelled back. He briskly walked across the room and out the door. Standing next to Gable on the deck he peered out over the vehicles. After a quick scan, he answered,

"Not my car, but thanks anyways." He then quickly turned and went back inside. Gable turned back towards the lot and stepped to the railing.

"Anything?" he asked.

"*Black Land Rover, keys are under the seat.*"

"Very good, Nell, very good"

Chapter 12

"I thought you said these men were competent, Captain Mitchell." Dr. Richards was visibly disappointed as he looked down at Captain Mitchell's cell phone on the desk. His eyes panned up to the man sitting in the chair opposite his.

"You can't expect me to control agents in the field thousands of miles away!"

"I can expect you to be responsible for them! Tell me Captain, how did he get all the way back to Buffalo by the morning." He stood from his plush chair and continued his rant before the Captain could answer. "I'll tell you how Captain, he obviously eluded you on the grounds last night and boarded a plane. Fan to the closest airport, something he could of reached on foot, check flights, inventory your vehicles, do something! I need him back!" His voice slowly elevated throughout the speech.

"What if it wasn't really him," he retorted.

"Is that what you're telling me, are you telling me that it wasn't him? Are you now telling me your men can't use their eyes, is that what you're saying!?" The stress of the situation was obviously building on him and Captain Mitchell took it as his cue to leave.

"I'll run down the leads and we'll bring him back, Doc. I've got this," he said as he eased from the chair and moved towards the door.

"See that you do Captain, see that you do." The Captain shut the door behind him and headed towards the exit.

Outside the silo there was a small curved roof hangar where the small militia kept its vehicles. Inside he personally inspected all the vehicles: three Hummers, a covered flatbed with boom, and two All Terrain Vehicles. All were accounted for. He went to the layout of the search grid, which was still drawn on a whiteboard in the rear of the hangar. Given the speed of a man on foot and the time that he was missing, the search grid should of more than covered it. He pulled out a sectional map from the glove box of one of the Hummers that clearly showed nearby airports. The only one that he could of made it to in the previous night and still had a chance of catching flights out of the area was the Fall River Mills Airport. He immediately dispatched Sergeant Pennyhall, one of his best men, with a picture of Gable Flagstaff to scour the airport. As he waited for the report back, he walked about the interior of the facility trying to think of other options.

"Maybe he was able to use the machine to get out," he thought. "Maybe he never left the building at all." He headed to the Chamber Room to look for evidence. Upon entering he noticed one of the technicians running routine tests on a laptop in the corner. The man looked up from his work long enough to give the Captain a nod, but then the Captain approached with a question.

"Tell me, can you see on there if the chamber was used last night?" he said as he pointed to the computer screen.

"It hasn't been used since we brought the second man through, sir. Are you wondering if he could have gotten out by using it?" he asked back to the Captain.

"I'm exploring all possibilities here."

"Well, it would be virtually impossible because the decompression chamber is necessary for proper arrival conditions. There would have to be another lab somewhere with their own chamber and they would need a fresh DNA sample from the subject. They would also need to know that he was here before they could pull him there. There's no other place like this in the country sir," the technician explained, "He didn't come through here, sir. I guarantee it."

Meanwhile back in Buffalo, Agent Douglas had pulled himself back thru the window in Gable's den and into the neighbor's yard before making that next call for an ambulance. He told them he'd been walking around his house and badly twisted his ankle. Believing he was the homeowner, they took him to the Emergency Department of the nearest hospital without question. Now he was being transported in a wheel chair to the X-Ray Department. The Emergency doctor thought initially he had a severe sprain, but had ordered x-rays to be sure. He was disgusted with himself for being so careless at the house; he partly blamed himself for Adam's untimely death.

"I should have noticed the laser system in the window, that was sloppy; rookie mistake," he said to himself. Their detail was to be completely covert, zero residual presence. He had hoped there would be a containment crew coming from the installation in California, but the sound of the Captain's voice made him doubt the possibility. If the police found Adam's body, they would most likely tie him to it and he'd never get back.

The orderly pushed him to the elevator and hit the 'up' button. As they waited for the elevator, she tried to make small talk.

"Well, we'll take you to the 4th floor and get that ankle x-rayed and then come back down here to the exam room. With luck you'll be out of here soon!" Douglas hadn't talked much thus far and really wasn't in the mood for chitchat.

"Great," he replied shortly as he sat slumped in the chair. The door opened to the extra deep elevator car as she spun him around and backed in. She pushed the button for the 4th floor and the door closed in front of them.

"So did you step in a hole or a bad spot in the yard?" asked the orderly still trying to make her patient feel better.

"Yeah, I stepped in a real bad spot."

"Well, I think we'll find it's not broken and you'll be back on your feet in no time. I've seen lots of breaks and I'll be willing to bet you're just a sprain."

"Well, I'll take your professional opinion on it," he said grumpily. The elevator only got to the second floor during the short conversation and came to a full stop. The door opened and two nurses entered pushing a hospital bed with a sleepy patient. Agent Douglas listened to the women's conversation.

"So after we get him in a regular room, let's go get something to eat."

"Sounds good to me, it should only take a few minutes to check my patient in. But after lunch I have to come back and deal with Mr. Flagstaff though. His family never signed the paperwork for his insurance, so it's probably going to be a pain."

"So his brother identified him and then took off, huh?"

"Yeah, weird though, I was heading into the observation room to give him the papers and I heard him talking to someone about a 'landing site' or something like that and when I turned the corner, there was no one there!"

"Strange," remarked the other nurse.

The elevator stopped at the next floor and the door opened. Douglas almost rolled out of the wheelchair when the nurses stepped out. He jostled around so much in the chair trying to get to his cell phone that the orderly thought he was having a seizure!

"Sir, are you ok?" she asked grabbing his shoulder. He ignored her as his fingers found the phone and pulled it from his pocket, flipping it open in one move.

"MITCHELL!" he yelled into the phone! As the phone dialed he rubbed his face with his free hand, "C'mon, c'mon!"

Back at the hidden facility, Captain Mitchell was leaving the Chamber Room after his disappointing conversation with the technician. His phone began to ring as he hit the elevator. He was in a bad mood already after finding no reportable leads; he was hoping this wouldn't be more bad news.

"Captain Mitchell," he answered as the elevator doors closed behind him.

"Captain, this is Douglas, I'm at the hospital; the hospital were the team dumped the brother! Sir, he was here, the target was here! Someone overheard him say he was going back to the 'landing site'. I think he's heading back towards you!" he exclaimed.

"Calm down Douglas, good work. Anything else? Was he with anyone?"

"Not sure sir, I never saw him. They say they thought he was talking to someone before he left. I can't confirm that. That's all I got sir."

"Ok, Douglas. So you gonna live or what?" he asked in a half joking, half serious tone.

"Yes sir, I think my ankle's sprained, but I'll make it back. We've lost Adams though."

"Adams who, soldier? You come back ASAP, you hear?" said the Captain as he stepped off the elevator into the office floor.

"Yes sir." The agent closed the phone as the confused orderly pushed him off the elevator onto the 4th floor.

"A joke my friends and I like to play sometimes," he said looking back at his helper, "we're just messing around." She nodded down to him as they pulled up to the registration desk. She stepped up to the attendant behind the high counter and said,

"He's all yours Carie!"

Chapter 13

Just before reaching Richard's office his phone went off again. This time it was Sergeant Pennyhall at the small airport just twenty miles north.

"No one has seen him here, Captain. I've got the local Five-O going through airport security tapes and I've shown his picture to all the lounge lizards. They all say they don't recognize him. For cover I'm telling them that he walked away from boot camp and we're looking for him. That should work for us, right?"

"Yeah, that'll be fine, but listen, I've got new information that he's coming back. I'm real sure he'll be coming near that landing site in the Yosemite area. I don't know if he's flying in or driving in but I want to grab him when he shows up. I'll assign eight men to you now, move in and canvas the small towns and little airports around that area. Call me immediately if you see any sign of him!"

After the man confirmed the orders, the Captain pressed the two-way radio function on the phone and ordered eight of his men to meet the Sergeant off-site and join the hunt. He then rounded the doorway directly into Dr. Richard's office. At the desk sat Richards typing away on his computer.

"I've got good news, Doc. He's coming back to California. We'll get him when he arrives." The doctor looked away from the screen and settled his eyes on the soldier moving to the chair across the office.

"Why on earth would he travel back here and how do you know this in the first place?" he calmly asked, easing his hands away from the keyboard.

"My 'competent' agent in the field, that's how," he said sarcastically. "He got a tip that Flagstaff is heading back to the landing sight, for what reason, I don't know." He had the doctor's full attention now.

"That's good news, Captain, so what are we doing to get him back? Tomorrow I have a meeting with our sources. I need results," he said plainly as he sat back into the tall chair.

"Don't worry," he replied. "I've got a few men scattered around the area; they'll see him when he comes around." The dispatched men were indeed on their way to the rendezvous to get their new assignments.

Meanwhile Gable and his companion rolled south to North Fork in their newly stolen vehicle. Unsure of their next step, Nell posed a question.

"What will we do when we arrive, Gable?" the voice asked inside his head.

"We'll have to do a little research. We'll look into anything strange that happened at the time your friend may have shown up; maybe we'll get lucky. This is only a hunch, Nell, so if nothing shakes out I'm really not sure where to go from here," he said trying to brace his new friend for the possibility of failure. The short silence in his head told him Nell was thinking about this prospect, so he continued, "But don't worry, this is a really good hunch!"

"If we fail it will only prolong my time here. I have been directed to not return without the cleric. However," the voice paused as if for intentional emphasis, *"they will continue to search for you and will most likely eventually use your brother to bring you out."* The voice ended.

"It's a good hunch Nell, this is right!"

The black Land Rover continued to roll down the road and shortly came upon the town of North Fork. It was an old logging town with a population of about 3,500 citizens who lived the simple small town life. There were only a few main roads through the town and since the logging mill had shut down years ago, it had been struggling ever since.

During the ride down, Gable had been thinking how he could conduct his investigation. He decided to say he was an author or was some sort of investigative reporter doing a story or something, he hadn't quite decided. He did figure he could save some time by going directly to the local police. He parked the vehicle up the street from the station.

"Can I help you?" said the officer behind the counter as Gable walked in.

"I hope so," said Gable trying to speak confidently. "I'm a reporter for a local magazine and I was wondering if you could help me out with some information. The piece I'm doing is kind of a reflective feature on events in our neighboring towns, mainly focused on over a decade old. Funny stories, news from the headlines of the day, stuff like that." He stopped his introduction and beamed at the officer. He was impressed with himself for conjuring up such a cover story on the fly.

"Well man, I'd like to help you, but I've only been here about six years.

Officer Chadwick's been here twice as long as I have. Hold on a minute." The officer left the counter and passed thru a door leading back to the locker area. A few moments later a different uniformed officer emerged and came around to the front of the counter to greet Gable.

"Good afternoon," he said extending his hand. "I'm Officer Jeremy Chadwick, I understand you're a writer of some sort?" Gable returned the gesture and gave back a firm handshake.

"Journalist, really," he said hamming it up. "I'm doing a piece on interesting stories and headlines from years ago, it's my editor's idea. I'm out doing a little research and talking to people today," he finished as he released his handshake. The policeman replied,

"That sounds like a fun job. What did you say your name was again?"

"I'm sorry, my name is Gable Flagstaff."

"You wouldn't happen to have any identification on you? I hope you don't mind me asking," said the officer apprehensively.

"Sure, that's no problem, I understand fully," he said as he reached into his pocket thankful he still had his old California license. After a quick look at his ID, Officer Chadwick motioned for Gable to enter a small lounge located off the main lobby. A coffee table with two couches centered the room. In the corner was a tall late model refrigerator with a short length of counter cabinets butted up to it on one side. Officer Chadwick stepped up to a countertop coffee machine and tossed some pocket change into a Styrofoam cup marked '25 CENTS'.

"Can I buy ya' a cup?" he asked over his shoulder at Gable who had found himself a seat on one of the couches.

"Sure," he replied. The man turned back and topped off two cups before sitting down at the other couch. He handed a cup to Gable and sat back into the cushions.

"Careful, it's hot stuff." He paused as he took a sip. "So you're looking for stories here, Gable?"

"Actually I've been told to focus on events of 1993." He smiled slightly. "My editor's got something for that year, not sure what his aim is, but as long as he signs the checks, right?" Gable chuckled lightly. "Anyways, he wants me to write about things that were out of the ordinary or interesting for that year."

"Just a workingman, huh. Well you're in luck. My first year in this department was 1993 and frankly my most memorable." The officer eased into a line of stories as if he'd been waiting for the opportunity to talk his whole life.

"I don't know if it's book material, but that was the year the Lafayette boys stole a semi truck, shot it up and drove it in the lake. It took a big rig and two divers to get that out, amazing how far they got that thing in." Gable had found a writing pad in the truck and had brought it in with him. He attentively took notes on whatever the officer was saying, as if everything was going into a very important article some day.

"Near the end of '93 the sawmill was winding down. Damn shame to lose that thing; by the start of '94 the mill cut its last log."

"Ok, I got it," Gable said quietly as he jotted on the pad. A few more stories were told before the information began to show promise.

"That was also the year the North Fork Bank's vault was taken clean, never did catch that guy. Amazing story, but you should ask Bob Kingston at the bank about that one. He's General Manager there now, but he almost lost his job that year. One hundred twenty thousand dollars in the middle of the day and no leads." But that was exactly the sort of lead Gable and his friend was looking for. He tried to get the officer to elaborate more but he seemed reluctant to talk about the failed investigation. A few more short stories and Gable was sure that he had the only lead that was going to help. He soon decided he should pay the banker a visit next. On the very next lull in Officer Chadwick's narration, he quickly stood up.

"Officer Chadwick, I want to thank you very much for your time. You've got a lot of good stuff in here," he said tapping his pad, "I think I'll head over to the bank and talk with Mr. Kingston, maybe get some more on that vault robbery thing." He put his empty cup in a trashcan next to the door and stepped into the small lobby. The policeman did the same and followed him out to the lobby double doors.

"Well, tell Bob I sent you over there. If you don't he's just gonna be calling over here when you start asking him about it."

"Sure thing and thanks again for the material." Gable shook his hand and then pushed through the first set of double doors into the vestibule. Just as his hands touched the push bar of the outside door, the officer pushed through the doors behind him.

"I can't believe I forgot about Frenchy!" he exclaimed.

"Excuse me?" Gable said as he spun his head back towards the man.

"Frenchy!" The officer let out a small laugh and continued on. "In '93 I picked up this foreign guy, at least most everyone thought he was foreign, he had a weird accent. He came strolling into town stark naked one day, said he was lost in the Park and somebody had taken his clothes. Strange fellow. Hung around the area for months just talking to everyone and doing little odd jobs. People just started calling him Frenchy because of the way he talked." Gable took his hands off the door.

"Was that before or after the robbery?" he asked excitedly.

"Kind of hard to remember. Totally unrelated stories though, Mr. Flagstaff. Why the interest?" he asked puzzled.

"Just trying to establish a time line. Thanks again!" Gable pushed open the front door and headed to the Land Rover. For the first time there was genuine enthusiasm in Gable's inner voice.

"*You think it was the Cleric?*" it said.

"Who else could it be, Nell! It all fits! I bet you anything that he took the bank vault for everything in it too."

Chapter 14

The bank was a small building all on its own with a rather plain looking street face. Gable parked in front and hustled to the door. Just inside the entrance there was a small half wall office off to the side; the nameplate velcroed to the wall read 'Bob Kingston'.

"Mr. Kingston?" he said as he poked his head inside the entryway of the office.

"Yes?" replied the man sitting behind the desk inside. "Can I help you?"

"I was hoping to have a few moments of your time if I could," Gable replied.

"If you're opening an account or have a problem with an existing account please see one of our specialists, or I'd be happy to help you if you have an appointment." Bob Kingston was trying to keep typing into his computer but could see that his visitor wasn't leaving.

"No sir, I'm not here for banking. My name is Gable Flagstaff and I'm a reporter, of sorts, and I'd like to take a few moments of your time and talk with you. Officer Chadwick said to tell you that he sent me over here." Gable pointed his thumb over his shoulder as if the policeman was behind him.

"Jeremy Chadwick sent you over? Well, you must be a man of importance then." Bob Kingston's demeanor seemed to change almost instantly as he stood from his desk and invited Gable into his office. "Come in, come in. Sorry for not inviting you in directly. They've put my office in a bad traffic spot here and I get everything from ATM problems to mortgage refinancing walking in my door. How can I help you?" The man motioned for Gable to sit in the only other available seat in the office.

"I'm doing a story," he said as he seated himself, "it's a story about stories really. Can you remember a man the town called Frenchy?"

"Wow, that's going back some time. Sure I remember him. He came through here over 10 years ago. Quiet fellow, hard worker."

"Hard worker? Did he work here?" Gable asked.

"Here?! Heavens no. Frenchy was a hermit! He did a lot of odd little jobs around town for money. I had him help me with some exterior work on my house once for a few days. Didn't seem to know anything about handy work, but I remember he picked things up real fast when you worked with him. I didn't mind helping him out. I remember he had a strange accent too." Gable was trying to contain his excitement. His luck was holding as the pieces continued to fall into place.

"Can you can remember what you talked about?" Gable asked.

"Jeez, mister, that was a long time ago. I was pretty new at the bank then, so I probably talked about work and probably the weather. You know, just small talk mostly I'm sure. I can't remember." Kingston paused. "Is that important?"

"Not really, I was just curious. Officer Chadwick also said there was a big robbery about that time. What can you tell me about that?" he questioned. Bob Kingston's face flashed a very serious glare back at Gable.

"So that's why you're really here, huh? Well, I had nothing to do with that, as it was proven back in '93," he said plainly. Sensing the defensiveness in his voice Gable reassured him that he was only doing light stories and wasn't placing blame. The manager seemed to calm and continued his account. "I was only a year or two at the bank and my main function at the time was to know the vault inside and out. I was responsible for all transactions and I took the responsibility very seriously, it was always on my mind. It was never fully discovered how the robbery took place, but they thought it looked like an inside job. So naturally they thought it was me."

"Again I apologize, Mr. Kingston, I didn't mean to bring up a bad memory," said Gable.

"That's ok, it's just sometimes that old story comes up and I have to be reminded of the whole thing. The funny thing was that our surveillance cameras in the lobby never captured anyone going in or out of the vault, but yet the whole thing was cleared out. So strange." He stared off as if he was remembering the day itself. Gable thought it was time to change the subject.

"So, what ever happened to that Frenchy guy?" Gable asked nonchalantly trying not to spike any suspicion.

"I'm not real sure. The way he was so quick to pick up on things and the fact that he didn't have anything to lose, I remember half jokingly saying he should make his way up to Reno and take up gambling. At the time a group of us used to have a poker night and I let him tag along once. No one could bluff that guy; I remember he took my stack pretty quick that night. He was around for a few months and then he was gone; never heard from him after that."

"Well, I hope everything worked out for the guy. Listen, Mr. Kingston, I appreciate your time." Gable slid forward and stood from his chair, Bob Kingston did the same.

"You're sure you have enough for your story?" the manager questioned as they shook hands over the desk.

"Oh yes Bob, it's coming together quite nicely. Thanks again!" Gable hastily exited the office and headed back to the vehicle.

Back at the police station, Officer Jeremy Chadwick was reading the first page of an interesting two-page fax. It was an All Points Bulletin about a military enlisted man that had wounded another soldier and had gone AWOL. It was in fact the false story that Sergeant Pennyhall had been concocting and spreading out in the area. The officer scanned the document briefly not really catching the name, until the second page slipped out onto the paper tray. It was a crystal clear image of Gable's California license with his name circled next to the picture. He caught one more word before dropping the paper on the floor and rushing out of the building: DANGEROUS.

By this time Gable and Nell were driving out of town discussing their successful research.

"This is great Nell, I'm convinced the Cleric came through here!" he said to himself as he drove past a sign that said 'Diner Up Ahead'.

"*So how do we follow his trail now? What's next?*" the voice answered.

"Next, Nell, is me eating at this Diner. I'm starved! I don't suppose you'll be ordering anything off the menu?" He chuckled as he pulled off the road into the small gravel parking lot.

"*I have sustenance in my ship that I prefer. I still struggle with the digestion of your food. I will transport there now and return to this vehicle,*" he said plainly.

"Take your time, I'm going to!" He hopped out of the Land Rover and strode across the empty parking spaces to the Diner door. The smell of simple home cooked food hit him as he opened the door. His stomach grumbled in delight almost immediately.

Meanwhile, outside the bank, Officer Chadwick was hurriedly questioning his friend Bob Kingston.

"He was just here 20 minutes ago, Jeremy! Are you sure you've got the right guy, he seemed genuine to me?" Bob said as he paced nervously on the sidewalk.

"I'm just telling you what the APB said! I've contacted the military and they said they were heading down here now. I've got to find this guy and keep him contained. Do you have any idea where he was heading?"

"He never said, Jeremy. He said he had all the information he needed for his story, whatever that meant now, and headed out of here in his Land Rover."

"Land Rover?" questioned the officer.

"Yeah, why?" replied the bank manager with a puzzled look.

"Black?" he asked as he took a step backwards towards his parked cruiser.

"I think it was, why, what's wrong?" By now the officer was quickly rounding the front of the car and heading for the door. He shouted back to his friend as he grabbed the door and flung it open,

"A black Land Rover was reported stolen from Bass Lake this morning, I'll bet you ten bucks he's driving it!" He then dropped into his car and took off down the street.

Chapter 15

He spent the next twenty minutes cruising the few streets that made up the town and then began to search the outskirts.

Gable was finishing up his sandwich when the waitress behind the counter took a phone call by the cash register. Given the short length of the bar it was impossible for Gable to not overhear her conversation.

"Hello Jeremy. Umm, yes, looks like him." She turned her back in an obvious attempt to hide her discussion. "Yes, yes I can do that. How long?...Ok." She turned around sharply and walked directly over to Gable's place setting.

"Can I get you another coffee, sir?" she asked nervously. Gable felt something was wrong and suddenly did not want to be there. He leaned back from the counter and waved off the refill. The waitress immediately followed with a quick run down of the pies that were homemade and sitting on the shelves behind her. By now he was sliding off the stool and pulling out his money for the bill. The waitress seemed desperate to keep him there.

"So are you visiting in the area or just passing through?"

"No maam, thanks for the lunch." He didn't even hear her question as he threw his cash on the counter between them. He suddenly felt as if everyone in the place was watching him, he had to get out. Unbeknownst to him, the only patrol car belonging to the town of North Fork was speeding towards him down the highway. Gable had pushed through the front door and was now in the seat of the stolen Land Rover. He let the gravel fly as he hit the pavement and headed away from North Fork.

"Nell?" he said to himself. "Are you hearing me?" no response. He flew under an overhead highway sign that read 'Fresno 20 Miles' and immediately thought if he could get into the city he might feel safer, but he would have to stay with the vehicle or else Nell wouldn't be able to transport to him. "Where the hell is he?" he thought.

Then a thousand yards behind him, red lights broke into view. The North Fork car had him in sight. Inside the car the officer was being patched through to Sergeant Pennyhall, who was already in route to the area.

"Sir, he's right in front of me! I've got him in my sight. Do you want me to push pursuit?" said the officer into the microphone. The transmission had been patched to Pennyhall's cell phone.

"I'm on the main highway to the west of you, I'm getting off now to intercept. We do not want him entering Fresno. Don't pressure him, just keep an eye on him, I'll be there very soon!" The Sergeant ended his call and immediately phoned Captain Mitchell.

"Captain, a local cop's tailing Flagstaff now and I'm five minutes away from joining the pursuit. He's just east of Fresno," said the Sergeant.

"Listen up Pennyhall, we can't let the locals detain him and we can't afford to have him running loose. If you can't get him stopped, put him off the road. I'm not going to let this civilian ruin my career. I don't care what the Doc says. Am I making myself clear, Sergeant?"

"Completely, Sir. I'll update momentarily." He closed his phone and clicked it into the holder mounted on the floor of his suburban.

Meanwhile, Gable could not figure out why the police vehicle was staying so far back. 'Maybe he's not after me, maybe this is coincidence,' he thought. He kept up his accelerated highway speed and focused on making it to Fresno. The road was not flat by any means and the curves and hills allowed the visibility of the pursuit car to be random. This further helped to play the illusion in his mind that he was not being followed, but it was soon to be confirmed.

The highway was littered with back roads and access roads on both sides. Every once in a while a glimpse of a parallel road would come into view and he thought he saw a white suburban keeping pace. Sometimes he just saw a wisp of dust coming from the side of the other road as if someone had swung a corner too wide or had lost control. Up ahead he could see where the side road ran into his at a perpendicular angle. He was roughly two hundred yards from the intersection when Sergeant Pennyhall's large white suburban appeared around a curve on the road. He was the same distance from the intersection as Gable and it was clear he was not slowing for his stop sign.

"Oh crap," Gable muttered as he mashed down on the gas. Half the distance now, it seemed like it was going to be a perfect collision. Gable eased over into the left lane and gripped the wheel hard with both hands. He was viewing the large oncoming vehicle at more of an angle to his right now, close now. It was happening in a split second but to Gable it was all moving slow. He looked out his right window at the big front-end only feet away. His body tensed and his face tightened up into a grimaced expression; he was braced for the impact.

The Sergeant spun the wheel of the suburban hard to the right, just missing the back corner of Gable's vehicle. The tires made a low whirring noise on the highway as the bumpers of the vehicles made crisp parallel lines between them. The gap was only inches as the Sergeant's vehicle's back end went off into the gravel on the left of the road. As he lost traction, the gap between vehicles quickly grew. Gable's hands trembled slightly as he spun his head to look behind him at the now sideways truck.

"NELL!" he yelled into the open space in the back of the Rover. "Where are you?!" He shifted back into the right lane of the highway and put his eyes to the road. The sizeable vehicle behind him sprang to life when the tires again regained traction on the pavement. The police vehicle now moved quickly behind it as the two cars pursued Gable down the highway. Panicked from the near miss at the intersection, Gable took the vehicle up to 85mph. The unevenness of the road and the top heaviness of the SUV allowed for little more.

As he rounded a curve in the road that led into a long straightaway, he saw that he had more problems. A semi pulling a car carrier was lumbering down the straight road. A ways beyond it he could see that the road once again turned to curves and hills, an impossible area to attempt a pass. If he could get around the car carrier before the road changed back, it would make it very difficult for his pursuers to follow. It might be the little time he needed to get away. Unfortunately for Gable, the soldier following in the big white truck realized the same thing and he had the determination to end the chase before the pursuit became more difficult.

As the three vehicles made their way towards the rolling obstacle, he could make out the cars that were on the truck. It was a load of used cars; he knew because the one furthest back on the bottom tier was the exact make and model of the one he owned a year ago: Ford Taurus. He instantly snapped out of the memory as the Suburban smashed into the back end, whipping his head into the rest of the seat. It was only part one of a two-step procedure, as he would momentarily find out.

"NELL!" he screamed at the windshield ahead of him. He was coming up on the load of cars quickly, only fifty yards away, he could see all the cars very clearly now as they shifted around on their ramps. If there was a time to pass this rig, it was now, but the sudden jolt from the truck behind him had taken his nerve and he was freezing up. In the side view mirror he could see the damaged white front-end move to his left and creep up slightly. The soldier had training and he was very good at performing the PIT maneuver at high speed. The first step was to rattle the cage of the suspect and then secondly push sideways on the rear of their vehicle. The resulting spin out would most likely break the drive train or stall the vehicle out, but at this speed and given the make of vehicle Gable was driving; a violent rollover was most assuredly going to occur. Suddenly a familiar voice played in Gable's head.

"*Why are we going so fast?*" it exclaimed with a puzzled tone.

"Where the hell have you been!" Gable frantically yelled.

Just then the front of the Suburban swung sharply into the side of Gable's stolen vehicle. The hit was well placed, directly behind the back tire of the Land Rover. The impact threw Gable against the driver door window, his left hand slipped off the wheel and into the door as well. The semi had just started into the first left hand curve of the now winding road and he knew he had missed his window. His last vision was of the car carrier and the back end of that car that he remembered so well.

The Rover's back end slid out gracefully to the right as the Sergeant followed through into the right lane, this was a textbook execution of his training and he actually felt proud. The Rover continued to turn until it was almost sideways on the highway. As it became perpendicular to the Sergeant's damaged vehicle, the left side of the Land Rover picked off the road. He watched as the vehicle entered into its first roll. It had a lot of speed when it lost control and it was going to be used up now. The undercarriage and gas tank flashed into view twice before the entire truck leapt from the road and made two tight spins in the air. The director's hiking gear and personal affects exploded out the windows. It had broken the axle on the first roll and now a back tire broke free and shot straight into the air. Parts and broken pieces continued to fly as the road veered left and the wreck traveled in a straight line off into a small overgrown grassland lined with forest. When the demolished auto touched off on the soft dirt, it tumbled end over end and came to rest on its top at the edge of the National Forest.

Back on the highway, the Suburban came screeching to a halt in the middle of the debris field with Officer Chadwick coming up quickly behind him. Sergeant Pennyhall calmly opened his door and stepped from his vehicle onto a broken piece of taillight, the crunch seemed to break the silence. The officer immediately came running up the side of the truck.

"What the hell did you do that for!!!" he yelled at the Sergeant dressed in fatigues. "We could have got him another way!" The microphone on his shoulder crackled with the voice of his dispatcher. He had called for an ambulance before he left his vehicle but had forgotten to call out location. He turned his head and with panting breathe spoke out their location according to the mile marker next to the vehicles. The soldier then very plainly replied to the officer before he was finished speaking.

"He had a gun and was going to fire at us. I was closer than you were, you didn't see it. I did what I needed to do for our safety."

"I guess it's safe now, huh!" The officer brushed by the military figure and dashed down into the high grass. Broken fragments of the vehicle lined the road and showed the way to the nearly unrecognizable heap of metal. He did not immediately follow the policeman down into the field, instead he calmly reached back into his vehicle, pulled his cell phone from the holder and flipped it open.

"Mitchell," he said into it. As the phone dialed he watched over the damaged hood of his truck at the other man making his way across the path mowed down by the rolling Land Rover.

"Captain Mitchell," the phone announced.

"Sir, there's been a development. Gable Flagstaff is dead," he waited for his superior's reaction to the news.

"Ok, fine we'll deal with it. Where are you now?" the phone asked.

"East of Fresno. Sir, I had to force a wreck out here and a local cop already called out for an ambulance. How do you want me to handle it?"

"Ambulance? Well is he dead or not?" asked Captain Mitchell.

"Oh I'm sure he's gone sir. There's not a chance he's survived this crash." Pennyhall looked around at all the pieces of glass and broken plastic on the road as he spoke. He could see in the distance the officer was now on the ground at the wreck.

"Then bag him before they get there and get your ass back. I'm sure the doctor's going to want to take him apart anyways," he said unemotionally.

"I've already taken him apart, that shouldn't be hard. What should I do with the local?"

"I want no loose ends, Sergeant Pennyhall. Tie them all and return. Do you understand?!"

"Completely, sir." He promptly ended the call and walked around to the front of his truck to look at the damage. The first strike had taken out the grill and smashed in the majority of the front end.

"Hey, I missed the head lights, it is my lucky day," he said quietly to himself as he reached behind him to a holster on his belt. He pulled forward a Kimber .45 cal and slid the action back to chamber the first round. He reached around again to holster the weapon and stepped down off the road into the grass.

"He's been ejected!" the officer shouted back to the Sergeant as he pulled himself off the ground. Sergeant Pennyhall sped up his step towards the wreckage.

"Well, he's gonna be in the grass here somewhere. Start looking around." He started panning his eyes through the grass near the line of debris as the officer searched the edge of the woods for any sign of the victim. After ten minutes of searching, the Sergeant called in two of the men in the area that had been dispatched to him. As soon as he ended his call, the ambulance that Officer Chadwick had called for arrived on scene. Sergeant Pennyhall shook his head at the sight of it. He wanted to be out of the area before any more people showed up; at least his men were near and would arrive within the hour.

Two paramedics exited the ambulance and ran up to the policeman who was now closer to the road. With their help, the men scoured the grassy debris field for quite some time before the Sergeant's men arrived. Two highway patrolmen also joined the investigation. The large party swept the area multiple times and still turned up no corpse. The three military figures soon felt uncomfortable as the investigation turned to them. The highway patrolmen wanted to know everything about the 'Private' they were after. The Sergeant stuck hard to his cover story as dusk started to settle and other authorities erected lights to illuminate the search into the woods. Soon it became apparent that there was no body to be found and Sergeant Pennyhall had to make the phone call that he was not looking forward to.

Chapter 16

The impact threw Gable against the driver door window, his left hand slipped off the wheel and into the door as well. The semi had just started into the first left hand curve of the now winding road and he knew he had missed his window. His last vision was of the car carrier and the back end of the Taurus that he remembered so well.

He felt the pressure of his invisible friend pushing him against the door as the Land Rover started to move sideways on the highway. His eyes were tightly shut, as he knew the rollover was coming; there was nothing he could do.

He re-gripped the wheel tightly and waited for the worst. The driver side quickly picked off the road and careened over the top. Inside, hiking boots and camping gear instantly became projectiles as they shot up to the ceiling and rolled forward with the motion of the vehicle. Glass rained through the cab as the shards inside fought to get out. Gable continued to hold the wheel, his eyes squeezing shut as groans slipped out of his gritting teeth.

The wreck launched itself into the air and down into the tall grass off to the right of the road. Gable felt himself lean to the right as the vehicle veered to the left. He began to open his eyes. The Rover continued to tumble up to the edge of the woods as Gable heard the faint sound of skidding tires. He hadn't let go of the wheel yet and his vision was blurry from the amount of pressure he had held his eyes shut with. Muffled sounds of metal racks and chains came to him from outside the vehicle. As his sight cleared, he instantly focused on the clean dash in front of him! He looked frantically side to side to catch his bearings. He could see metal struts and dangling chains all around the car, and he was moving! He quickly realized he was on the car carrier heading away from the accident!

He then spun in the seat just in time to see the police car sliding up behind the damaged Suburban already stopped on the road. The parked vehicles disappeared around the bend; the driver of the rig oblivious to the destruction and chain of events that had just happened behind him. Gable turned back around and sunk into the seat of the Ford, putting his hands over his face.

"Gable, how did they find us so quickly?" said Nell. Gable was visible shaken from the experience and returned no comment. *"Are you injured, Gable? Please speak to me,"* Nell urged.

"Injured? INJURED, NELL??!! For God's sake I was almost killed! These guys mean business and I don't think they care anymore if I make it through this!" His hands were away from his face now and somewhat waving frantically as he spoke straight into the steering wheel. He felt only a little shake in his hands, like he always did when he felt panicky. This time however it wasn't near as bad as he thought it should be.

"Give me a minute here ok," he said as he tried to calm himself, "where the hell did you go anyways?"

"As I said, I required nutrition from my ship. We had agreed to, as you said, 'take our time' which I did."

"Well, take a little less time next time, all right! Christ!" The car carrier continued on unsuspectingly with its stowaways aboard. It passed through Fresno and jumped on Highway 99 heading North towards Sacramento. During the long ride on the highway, Gable pondered his next step. He thought back to what the banker in North Fork had said about Reno. A man who could read thoughts would be quite successful in a gambling town like that. In either case it was worth a shot, he thought.

"*Reno then,*" the ghostly voice echoed as it scanned Gable's mind. He often forgot about Nell's capabilities and the intrusion was still taking some getting used to.

"Yes, Nell," he replied through his thoughts, "if your Cleric shares your abilities as you say he does, he should be the biggest winner in town. I wouldn't be surprised if he's sitting there right now in the biggest house on the hill. I know if I could read minds in a game of poker, I'd never leave."

"*But the Clerics are among the intellectual elite in our society. I cannot imagine he would be content to remain there. Protocol states that if we are forced to land that contact must be established as soon as possible. I believe he would have to come back to his ship to send us a signal, I myself have contacted my kind every new moon since I've been here. Equipment in the ship is used to amplify our abilities, and permits a short burst of mental energy to travel the distance.*" Gable listened to Nell's thoughts and then replied out loud.

"But you said the ship was destroyed during the crash landing, right?"

"*Once the hull was breached, the Nitrogen levels in your atmosphere would have begun to deteriorate the equipment. It should still have functioned properly for a short time after the breach though, and I don't believe a Cleric would suspend his efforts for contact.*"

"But Nell, maybe it was damaged beyond repair, there's no way of knowing. Don't worry, friend, we'll find him. We'll get to Reno and find some place to sleep for the night. Tomorrow will be better, I'm confident they've lost our trail and there's no reason they should suspect Reno." He tried to comfort his friend, but did truly believe they were on the right track once again. It was beginning to get dark outside, but with luck the semi would take them all the way into

Reno. But luck hadn't been Gable's friend for quite a long time.

Although it had gotten dark, he had been watching signs for Route 80 East, which would take them to Reno. He had just noticed the sign for the entrance to the ramps, but the truck was in the wrong lane! He sat up in the seat of the car and peered out the window trying to find some sign that he was mistaken. The semi-truck's bright headlamps headed left down a lane marked 'San Francisco 60 Miles', it was confirmed, they were heading the wrong way!

Gable couldn't afford to waste time. He had to think fast. Ideas in his head flashed of movies he saw where heroes drove off the back of car carriers and escaped down the highway. It looked easy, they yanked a chain, pulled a lever, bang, and the car comes right off.

"*You can do that?*" Nell's voice sounded.

"Are you nuts?!" he answered back staring at the center of the steering wheel, "I can do this!" Gable pressed his palm hard into the steering wheel. Up in the cab, the driver heard the loud continuous noise of a car horn sounding off behind him. He swerved lightly in his lane trying to catch a glimpse of the headlights of the annoying driver behind him. It took surprisingly a few minutes to realize that the loud horn was coming from the cars on the carrier, but after figuring it out he quickly pulled over on the major highway. As soon as the rig came to a rest, the noise stopped.

"Nell, back on the ramp there was a little patch of trees in the grass between the highways. Did you see it when the headlights turned?" The driver was walking down the side of the carrier now.

"*Yes,*" was the simple reply. Gable slid down low in the seat as the man climbed up on the middle of the carrier. He could easily make out the man moving about the rig, as cars in the oncoming lanes showed his large outline. He had a flashlight out and was inspecting each vehicle, starting from the front.

"We need to go there, Nell," he whispered as he sunk as low as he could in the seat.

"*But Gable, it was dark, and I only saw it for a moment.*" Nell's voice got very serious. It reminded him of the first time the ghostly voice spoke to him and it made him a little nervous. The man moved to the second car back on the first level, the Taurus was only two more away.

"Nell, we have to get to Reno. If you put us in the clearing then we can walk off the highway and get another car. Let's just go!" he strained to keep his one way conversation a whisper.

"*But Gable, that's just it. It wasn't really a clearing, I didn't get a good look at it.*" The man was now at the car in front of Gable. He snaked his way through the second tier supports and the uneven ramps until he was shining his flashlight through its back window.

"I'm not sure I want to find out what happens when this guy discovers me, Nell!" He continued to whisper lightly as he slumped in the seat. He watched as the burly truck driver swung around his heavy Mag-Lite, inspecting the forward vehicle. He suddenly finished his check and spun around to the Ford Taurus. The concentrated beam of the heavy-duty light cut through the windshield and the half moon of exposed steering wheel and struck Gable in the eyes like a deer in the headlights. The surprised driver faltered back in the dark space between the cars and bumped into the trunk behind him.

Gable's eyes were open wide staring back into the light, and the truck driver was frozen with the Mag-Lite centered squarely on the stowaway. The driver yelled out, "HEY!" but it was hard to tell who was scaring whom. He took his first step to regain his balance, and the man in the car vanished in the light of the beam. If only he would have known that the man behind the wheel had instantaneously appeared a few miles back in between the highways, it may have stopped him from fainting onto the hood of the car.

Chapter 17

"AHHHHH!" Gable screamed as he quickly put his hand over his mouth. He was among the small trees that he had seen in the truck headlights as it had turned, but there was something wrong. His foot felt like it was frozen to the ground! He instantly started breathing hard as he looked down at his left foot hidden in the grass. His hands searched frantically in the dark and quickly bumped into something hard in front of his leg. It was a half-inch rebar stake that had been put in the ground to mark a drainage pipe! He grabbed hold of the swaying rod and followed it down to the ground, but it ended on top of his shoe! He realized the pain was only when he moved his foot, and it became immediately clear that the rod came directly up through his foot!

"Nell, Nell," he painfully whispered, "Oh God! What am I going to do?" He tried not to wiggle around but as a car went by, the lights trickled through the small trees around them giving glimpses of the horrible sight.

"I was afraid of something like this. Do you think we'll be able to continue tonight?" Nell asked calmly with a tone of sarcasm.

"CONTINUE?! You are nuts! Nell, there's a metal stake through my foot!" Another car went by and he quickly looked down at his dilemma. The rod looked as if it was growing straight right out of the top of his shoe. He tried to control his breathing and convince himself that he was in no immediate danger.

"Nell, I'm going to need a hospital. Do you understand?" He was talking out into the darkness hoping that his friend would understand the situation. After a long pause, his friend sounded back.

"*A hospital? Like your sibling? Gable, we cannot lose the time. I agree we will not make it there this night and I cannot transport us there, fore I have never been. You need to rest. Let me help.*"

"My foot, Nell! I need a doctor!" he whined back at the uncooperative ghost in the darkness.

"*You need the Remedial, and then rest!*" his words were as persistent as ever. Gable heard the footsteps in the grass this time as Nell stepped near and squeezed both his shoulders tightly.

Suddenly the cool ambient light in the room blinded Gable's eyes and he instinctively brought his hands up to his face to shield himself.

"*Your eyes will adjust if you let them, friend,*" said the voice. Gable felt someone hold his wrists and force them down allowing the light to hit his face. He slowly released the tight squint as his pupils adjusted to the light. As the vision cleared he could see a dark figure standing directly in front of him, and holding his arms! Was this Nell? The figure was just as tall as an adult man, but there was something different. He blinked hard a few times and the blurriness faded. His eyes only had to focus for a split second before he quickly wrestled his arms free and stepped back on his left foot. Excruciating pain shot up his leg as he screamed and dropped to the floor. He pulled his leg up to his chest and rolled to his side in agony.

"You're one of them!! You're one of those creatures that they killed on the ridge!" he yelled. It was true that the same hollow features existed in the creature's face: the horizontal oval eye lobe, the vertical elliptical shape that centered its face. But Nell's skin was much darker and he was shorter and less muscularly developed than the other beings that Gable had encountered.

"*I contest, Gable. The Braxton are a much underdeveloped species compared to the Nell. They have a purpose and they serve it,*" he paused, "*but I don't think now is the time to resort to name calling.*" Nell was trying his particular brand of humor again, and once again at the wrong time.

Gable looked over his knee at the shoed foot and the obvious small hole in the top of it. He pressed his lips together, took a deep breath, and then quickly slid off the shoe. He let out a painful murmur at the sight of the bloody sock. As he let his heal slowly down to the floor, it made a blatant red skid mark on the clean floor. Nell walked over and kneeled next to Gable.

"*Don't worry, Gable, the Remedial will heal you,*" he tried to say comfortingly.

"Where are we, Nell?" he said as he cocked his head around.

"*Well, you are in my craft. You needed healing and you assuredly needed rest. There is no way for them to find us here, even if they did, there's nothing they could do about it.*" There was a hint of arrogance in his voice as he stood up from the floor. Gable looked up at the dark face and asked,

"And why is that?"

"*Because this ship is impenetrable,*" he answered as he raised his arms from his sides seeming to invite Gable's eyes to look around.

The ship was splendid. The floor was clean and creamy white and the size of the room was at least double what he expected it to be. He could see no apparent operator's panel, and no furniture of any sort. The ceiling was curved as he would have imagined and it flowed into the walls and down to the floor almost seamlessly. On the walls, in what looked like random placement, there were different shapes of color. He could not make out defined edges of the shapes, but he surmised they must have had something to do with the operation of the ship. Nell strode over to the wall closest to where Gable laid and pressed his three-fingered palm against a dark colored shape on the wall that looked like a puddle of spilled paint. Suddenly, beneath it, a rectangular line formed in the wall and a solid shelf slid out from it.

"*This is the Remedial. It will undue all the damage to your limb.*" The voice was still sounding in Gable's head, Nell's face never showed any expression. His hand remained firm on the colored blotch as he looked over his shoulder down at his wounded friend.

"*You didn't think I'd travel 12 billion light years without a doctor, did you?*" Gable thought if Nell could have laughed, he would have at that moment. He watched as he slid his palm slightly on the wall and a strange pale glow came from the bottom of the protruding ledge. His foot was throbbing with every heartbeat and he could see that he was losing blood onto the ship's floor. Nell seemed unconcerned and very calm.

"*Can you position your limb beneath the Remedial light?*" Nell said. Without comment, he slid his bloody heal the few feet to the wall until his leg was under the glow. The rectangle, that was roughly two by four feet, instinctively slid down the wall and stopped only inches from the top of his foot. A warm sensation came over his leg, as if he had just stepped into a calm hot tub. He lie back on the flat floor and took a relaxing breath.

"It's warm," he said slowly.

"*It will heal you. You need to rest, it's very late.*" Nell stepped from the wall and walked to a different group of colored shapes and pressed both palms against a yellowish pair at hip level. The ceiling of the ship faded to transparency, as if Gable were watching clouds move out of a night sky. The transparency continued onto the walls and stopped at a fuzzy line on the floor. The ship was in a dark room, dimly lit by lights on the floor. It was the Clean Room that had been built on the side of the silo to house the ship, since the landing a year ago. It felt like they were on a floating bright plateau in the middle of the room. The Remedial now seemed to hang silently in mid air as it went to work mending his foot.

"Isn't that a little risky?" Gable said as he propped himself up on his elbows. He was quickly getting used to the strange sight of Nell as he walked about the floating surface.

"From the exterior the hull still appears solid, we are completely intact." He seemed to brush off his question as he continued.

"The first few weeks I spent inside this ship just observing your kind. Every day they would come to this room dressed in puffy gowns and rubber gloves and attempt to breech my hull. I've seen them try everything from vibration to flame, your species' persistence is quite impressive." Nell was facing out past the faded walls and into the room of the facility.

"It's that persistence ironically which brought us here. We knew that without halting your efforts, you would one day discover our kind. Perhaps the Higher Clergy was wrong though. Since venturing from this facility I've seen that not all of your kind is as they fear. Do you think perhaps one day there will be a peaceful coexistence?" He slowly turned his hollow face back at Gable.

"*Gable?*" Only the light snoring answered his question.

Chapter 18

The radio observatory was all a buzz. Earlier that afternoon personnel were out on the Allen Telescope Array (ATA) pad cleaning the first dish for the inspection. Inside the compound, system engineers were now running routine tests on the positional drives and electrical systems of the new array. Tomorrow would be the day of another customer inspection and Neil Allen was that customer. Dr. Richards recognized the activity around the area but by design was never involved. The information firewalls between programs kept a lot of things confidential and separated.

He instead remained behind his closed door throughout the day and worked on his budget proposal for Senator Brandt and his silent partners. He somewhat resented the other program that was running out in the open. The project manager wasn't even a doctor or student of science; he was an ordinary contractor working a build job. The real brain of the operation was the customer and sponsor himself and everyone knew it. During inspection it was not out of the ordinary for Mr. Allen to quiz some of the techs or ask the positioning operators to make practice moves with the simulation program. Once the project completed, all the radio dishes would have to be positioned in unison to achieve the maximum range of the device as a whole. He had invested millions and needed the program to be a success.

Dr. Richards imagined how much easier it would be to have a funding sponsor that cared as much about the process as they did the results. For him, that wasn't the case. Senator Brandt and his partners had been breathing down his neck for months about results and return on their investment.

They had a man they wanted to launch into the White House and the harnessing of the extraterrestrial power was going to be the platform; that is if he could ever figure out how to harness it. He would have to convince them that he really had a plan forward and had new avenues of research, or else the funding was going to stop. He knew the "boys on the hill" wouldn't want to be linked to extraterrestrial research, especially if it was a failure. He needed Gable. He needed his testimony that the latest landing was truly of the same species of creature that they've been keeping alive for twelve years, and of equal importance would be all the pending tests he had in mind for him. While the thought was fresh, he picked up the phone on his desk and contacted Captain Mitchell.

"So where's my man, Captain?" he asked the officer on the phone.

"Doctor," he started very seriously, "we have a problem. I believe the target has acquired the ability to transport." There was a long pause as the doctor absorbed what he'd been told.

"Are you insane, man?" he retorted to the Captain. "What do you mean?!"

"I mean we had him dead to rights and the only way he could have escaped is if he was able to transport like the machine can do. Maybe that creature we destroyed the night on the ridge passed its ability to him or something. I don't know, you're the doc!" he said disgustingly.

"Then why wouldn't he display those powers while under surveillance? If what you say were true, then that would explain how he escaped this building! Why would he suddenly begin to use the ability only now?" There were silent moments and then he erupted with an explanation, "Of course, the ship! Possibly bringing him in the vicinity of the ship could have triggered some reaction. It only makes sense that the creatures might draw power from it and therefore it may have activated the power for him! Most interesting!!" he paused again and then continued. "Did you say 'dead' to rights? Captain, it is even more imperative than ever that Gable Flagstaff be captured alive. He might be the key we're looking for!" The Captain quickly shot back,

"Let's say for a second that I am right about this, well then how the hell am I supposed to take him alive if he can just transport away?" He sensed his job was getting increasingly more difficult.

"I won't tell you how to do your job, Captain, but I'll tell you what I will do. I'll move the ship! If he did indeed gain his power from the ship, then he might need to renew that power by coming back to it. I'll simply move it and then we might be able to capture him here."

"Sounds too simple. You do what you need to, I'm going to hope my man missed something and our target's still out there. We'll talk in the morning, Doctor."

"Yes, in the morning, Captain Mitchell." He ended the call and eased back in his tall chair. He wondered to himself about the possibilities of his research if Gable was in confinement and he could transport like he knew the creature in the box could. He would have something then, they wouldn't be able to deny that. He did confess to himself that the possibility was against all odds, but in the morning he would have the craft pulled out of the building and stored in a storage hanger across the flat. They would complain, he was sure, about taking the craft out in the daylight and the very idea of storing it under a tarp in a dirty hanger didn't sit well with him either. Since it was brought to the facility it had been kept in a clean room environment where only scientists with gowns and gloves had come near it.

Still, because of that fact, no one would ever suspect it to be hidden under a dirty tarp in the back of a storage hanger, and that's exactly what Dr. Richards wanted.

Chapter 19

Morning seemed to come quickly for Gable; it was one of his most relaxing nights' rests in a long time. The awakening left something to be desired.

"*Gable,*" said a soft voice in his head, "*it's time, we must go.*" He slowly opened his eyes to Nell looking directly at him from only a few feet away. He jumped suddenly at the sight and banged his knee up into the still suspended Remedial.

"Jeez, Nell, you gotta be so close? You scared the hell out of me!" He pulled his leg out from beneath the dark object to rub his knee and saw the amazing sight. Not only was his wound healed but also his sock had been mended such that he couldn't even tell there was ever a hole at all. "That's amazing!" he exclaimed.

"*There is nothing amazing about it, Gable,*" said Nell as he stood up straight and pressed his hand to the invisible wall over the Remedial. "*The Remedial is a retro-replicating atomic manipulator, no more.*" An outline of the strangely shaped button appeared only for a moment and the Remedial rose upward and slid away into thin air. "*What is amazing is this.*" He swung his arm upward and followed its direction with his large dark eye. Above him was just as it was the night before; a transparent hull of a ship sitting in a large dimly lit room.

"Hey, is it even morning?" Gable questioned as he leaned forward on the floor.

"*For over three hundred rotations of your planet, every morning they have come to this room to scrutinize and clean in gowns and masks. This day there is nothing. Can you explain?*" He looked down at Gable who by now was helping himself off the floor.

"Vacation? Shift change? Maybe they just think your ship is boring, huh?" He shot Nell a joking glance, which seemed to ricochet on his unemotional face. By now he was used to Nell's lacking sense of humor. He looked down at his foot while he rocked back and forth, shifting his weight from heel to toe. "Heck of a machine you have there, even the blood's off my sock!"

"*Maybe it thought your sock was boring,*" said the voice in monotone. As Gable looked up with a smirk, Nell turned and walked towards the far edge of the bright floor. His hands reached out in mid air as the pair of yellowish pads became visible again before him. As he laid his palms firm on the colors, the walls began to materialize starting at the edges of the shiny floor and creeping to a point on the ceiling, once again bathing Gable in the intense bright light.

"Ahhh, could have warned me," he said as he covered his eyes and began peeking through his fingers trying to find his shoe.

"Oh crap." He picked it off the floor and looked through the hole, which started in the center of the laces and straight through the soul of the shoe, a perfect half-inch diameter. He grimaced as he slid it on.

"*Are you ready?*" Nell asked as Gable stood to face him.

"Yeah," he answered looking down through his shoe at the little circle of clean sock, "but can we go a few feet to the right this time?" Before he had a chance to look up, they were gone.

A few seconds later, the overhead floodlights of the Clean Room bathed the ship like a football stadium. Dr. Richards came bursting through the entry door of the room barking orders; a man in a clean room garment, mask, and rubber gloves was close on his heals.

"Dr. Richards, I understand that you are the director of this operation, but I implore you to reconsider! This ship hasn't been..." Dr. Richards cut him off directly.

"I have considered and reconsidered, Mr. Madison, and this is going to happen." He stepped in close as if to make his point and then turned back to the ship. The ship was set up on an enormous dolly that had large double swivel wheels all around the outside. At the end of the room the tall wall was actually an extremely large double door that led to another room, which served as an airlock to the outside. The doctor looked up to a long string of windows in the opposite wall about twenty feet off the floor where the control room actually was. He pointed back at the double door and gave them a thumbs-up. The doors parted slowly and very quietly as a propane-powered fork truck entered from the next room. Dr. Richards turned to face the man standing behind him. As he spoke, the exterior doors sounded off from the next room allowing a rush of wind and dust to slide across the super clean floors. Since the day of the crash the spacecraft had never left this room nor had that door been reopened, the man in the mask stood in amazement.

"Storage hanger, tarp, are we clear Mr. Madison?" He bent down slightly to look directly into the mask. "Are we clear?" he repeated.

"Whatever you say, Dr. Richards," he said disgustedly as he pulled the protective mask off his face.

"Excellent, I appreciate your cooperation," the doctor said as he promptly turned and walked toward the morning light of the open doors. Behind him the fork truck had already connected to the big dolly's hitch and was starting to pull.

When Agent Douglas reported that Adam's was still at the house in Buffalo and had been killed, Captain Mitchell knew he'd have to act fast before any local authorities got involved. He had called a contact totally outside his military unit, a man that cleaned up 'messy' jobs for him in the past. The man worked thru a foreign bank account and never left a trace, whatever the cost. He had just received word from the 'cleaner' that he had to burn the house! Whether it was necessary or not, he trusted that it needed to be done. He had no remorse over the fact that Gable Flagstaff had just lost every possession he'd ever owned in a fire thousands of miles away and was happier about tying up loose ends.

The report from Sergeant Pennyhall the night before had distressed him enough to make him want to personally drive down to North Fork and assist in the investigation. That morning he decided to do just that. Just in case his theory was correct about Gable and his teleporting, he was going to take some precautions.

He secretly went up to the Chamber Room before leaving and spoke with the technician he had met the other night.

"So if I want to use the machine to come back here quickly, what do you need from me?" he asked the tech.

"Keep in mind sir that we believe the creature is not doing well and we're not sure how many more transports we can get out of him. My guess is one more long distance transport and we're gonna fry him for good."

"Save it techy, it's worked for years. What do you need from me to bring me back in a hurry?" he asked persistently.

"Well, I need a DNA sample not more than 24 hours old, and I need to know your location globally within 10 square meters," the tech answered very plainly.

"Fine. My phone has GPS capability. If I call you, you bring me back ASAP." He plucked a hair from his head and put it in a bag the obviously annoyed technician had already opened for him. "I'm counting on you," he said as he stepped from the desk and over to the elevator. He pushed the button impatiently and a few moments later stepped in.

Within thirty minutes the officer was on Highway 5 heading south towards the small town of North Fork. Sergeant Pennyhall had sold the local authorities on his fake story of Gable being a dangerous military criminal and the empty search at the roadside concluded that he must have survived and escaped. Sergeant Pennyhall saw the wreck first hand and knew that wasn't the case.

Early that morning he and his men had ventured into town and were carrying on their own investigation. He had sat with Officer Chadwick and listened to the tale of Gable being a reporter and asking the officer all sorts of question about events long past. Officer Jeremy Chadwick had told the Sergeant that Gable also spoke with Bob Kingston at the bank and he went to question him next.

"So he was asking about a 'Frenchy' character?" he said to the bank manager while sitting in the small office to the side of the lobby.

"Yes, he seemed particularly interested in that," he answered.

"Who was this Frenchy? He lived here I understand."

"He was just some homeless person that the town took a liking to for a short while. He was here for months before running off somewhere. That was over ten years ago, I was surprised the young man even cared. Me and that reporter, or whoever you say he was, only talked a few minutes and then he took outta here in a hurry it seemed," said Mr. Kingston.

"Did he give you any idea where he was heading?" he asked probingly.

"Nope, he never said. He was more interested in Frenchy. I do remember him asking where I thought Frenchy had disappeared to; I told him I thought Reno."

"So what's the connection with this 'Frenchy' guy and Flagstaff?" questioned the Sergeant as he tapped his short pencil on the little pad in his hand.

"I wouldn't know, sir. If you'll excuse me though I would like to get back to work," he said as he glanced over to the stack of papers in a plastic tray marked 'IN'.

"Of course," said the Sergeant springing to his feet, "thanks for your time and cooperation." He reached over the desk and shook the still seated manager's hand.

"I sure do hope you've got the wrong man, Sergeant. Mr. Flagstaff seemed like a genuinely nice person," the banker said looking up.

"Rest assured Mr. Kingston, he's our man. You try to have a good day now." He released the man's hand and turned out the office door out onto the sidewalk. He reached into his pocket and took out his cell phone to inform the Captain of the strange news.

"What the hell was he up to, Sergeant?" said Captain Mitchell.

"I have no idea, sir," he answered.

"That was around the time that the first ship came down in Yellowstone. I wonder if there's a connection?" Mitchell paused, "Do you know where he's heading?"

"Nahh, he didn't tell these locals anything. He was asking a lot about that homeless guy and they think that guy went to Reno! Maybe he went there, who the hell knows." Pennyhall was pacing on the sidewalk waving his free hand in frustration. "What do you want me to do here?"

Captain Mitchell was just south of Sacramento when he'd gotten the Sergeant's call. He headed towards the very next exit.

"You gather your men and head to Reno. I'm two hours west of there now. It's the only lead we've got and we're running out of time. You call me when you hit the city." He flew up the next off ramp and whipped his car around to the northbound entrance. In a few hours he would be in the Biggest Little City in the World, Reno.

Chapter 20

Hours before, Gable and his once again invisible friend had appeared safely this time in the clearing by the highway. He looked off to his left at the rebar stake still in the ground and got an eerie chill. Through the thin scattered trees he could see a minivan only a big hundred yards east parked on the side of the highway.

"What do you think Nell?"

"Three females. I believe they are very happy inside, surprising given that one of their tires is deflated," he answered.

"Women in distress," Gable said with confidence, "I think we just found our ride, c'mon." He emerged from the grassy depression and walked briskly down to the troubled vehicle. As he approached, he clearly saw there were three women inside; all elderly women all dressed up for the day. He was only a few car lengths away when the passenger spotted him walking up in the side mirror. The lady promptly stuck her head out the window, almost knocking off the large red hat she was wearing.

"Yoo-hoo," she wailed, "are you from the motor club?"

"No maam, just making my way to Reno." She tucked herself back inside as he strode up to the passenger window.

"Reno? That's where we're going!!" said the driver who seemed very excited. "We've been planning this trip for months! We're going to win big!" she said as she tapped a handbag bulging with change. "Just as soon as our flat is fixed, we'll be on our way. Harriet called the motor club already with her cell phone." She thumbed behind her to the middle seat of the van at an older lady jubilantly waving a cell phone.

"Well, my good ladies, I can tell that you will indeed be big winners today. I wish you could get there sooner," he said as he stepped back from the vehicle and looked down the long highway.

"I could use a little help here Nell" he thought to himself.

"*Of course,*" he stated. There was a pause as he offered a little persuasion in the driver's ear.

"Young man! I have an idea!! If you'd be so kind as to change our tire for us we could give you a ride there with us! Oh, that'd be grand!" she said with a large smile.

"I accept your proposal, maam. Is the jack and tire in the back?" he asked stepping towards the window again.

"Yes, yes, it's all there. Now thank you very much!" The lady in the seat behind the driver waved her cell phone in the air mockingly. The driver turned slightly and retorted,

"Well then you can just call them back on your fancy phone and tell them we can take care of ourselves!" Gable lifted the hatchback and removed the spare tire and jack from the back floor of the van and within twenty minutes the minivan was heading east on its way on highway 80 towards Reno. For the next hour and a half Gable sat in the far rear seat listening to the older women's theories on slot machines and gambling. They were a happy bunch; each had extravagant red hats and acted very excited over the littlest of things. They seemed very self absorbed in their conversations and at times he wondered if they remembered that he was still in the van. But soon they did.

"So young man, what's your name? Are you a gambler?!" they asked with animation. "What are you heading to Reno for?"

"Well, my name is Gable, Gable Flagstaff. I've got to meet a man there, or rather I've got to find a man there. A friend. A friend of a friend really," he said nervously.

"Is he a gambler, because we're going to Silver Legacy Resort Casino; the biggest casino there. You look like a card player. We play the One Armed Bandits!" said the lady in the middle seat as the three of them burst out giggling.

"I'm really not much of a card player." Gable was telling the truth. He had only recently been introduced to Texas Hold'Em on the Internet and he didn't fair well his first few times in. "I've played a little poker here and there, but that's it."

"Maybe you can show us how when we get to the Silver! Maggie plunked a bunch of quarters on one of those green tables once and they made her leave!"

"Umm, sure," answered Gable uncomfortably. It wasn't very long after that they arrived in Reno. The ladies went thru a drive thru window and they all had something to eat in the van while they sat in the parking lot of the casino.

"You've got to keep your strength up. When you face the Bandits for 6 hours, you can't get up," said the driver. No sooner did she end her sentence did the passenger pick up the line.

"That's right! You never want to give up your machine before the big payout!" Gable was just happy to eat something. Through this whole ordeal he had barely eaten and only thought about finding this Cleric and getting his brother out of the hospital. These ladies seemed to take his mind off things if only for a short time.

"Let's go ladies," announced the driver, "You too Mr. Poker Player!" The doors opened and the red hatted ladies flowed out like sap from a pine tree. Gable thought it was quite comical for all the talk they had put out on the way there, either way he helped them all into the casino. As they entered the casino, a Greeter at the door further helped the ladies inside.

"Welcome ladies!" he said. The Greeter had seen this scene before and knew what to do. "Can I show you to the slots?"

"No sir, we're going straight to the poker tables. We've got a player with us today and we're going to win big, I can feel it!" She stepped lightly to the side as the Greeter got his first look at Gable who was helping the last of the ladies up the steps.

"So you're the ace in the whole, huh," he said, humoring the ladies. Gable looked up with a surprised expression.

"Uh, not really," he replied.

"Well let's get him on a table, shall we ladies?" The three old ladies seemed to come alive with a burst of excitement. Gable thought they were just more excited that someone was actually catering to them. They grabbed his arm and led him straight onto the floor. Among all the flashing lights and loud noises of the casino the three brightly dressed women in their boisterous hats seemed to fit right in. The greeter gave him four 5-dollar chips courtesy of the house as he led them up to a five dollar minimum bet Poker table and sat him down.

"Now sir, don't let these ladies down!" He patted him on the shoulder and returned to the door with a slight smirk on his face. Gable wanted to pursue his quest to find the Cleric, but he thought having a little fun along the way couldn't hurt. Nell had a different opinion.

"How will this help us, Gable?" the voice muttered as Gable scanned the table.

"It's a slight diversion, Nell. We have time, just relax. I'm thinking this is probably what your Cleric friend did years ago to survive so let's consider it research." Gable was talking in his mind and forgot the dealer was waiting for him.

"Sir, are you in?" the pretty girl behind the table asked.

"Oh, yes, yes I am." He threw in his chip and received his cards. Not bad, he thought. He found a pair of twos in the hand and looked over at the other players. At the table were two other men. One looked like an insurance salesman and the other appeared as if he was on vacation and hiding from his wife. The play went quick with no betting until all three cards had been overturned in front of the dealer; all junk except for his one pair. The family man almost immediately folded out. The salesman on the other hand confidently threw in a few more chips to bring his contribution to 20 dollars; he apparently had a strong hand. Gable was just about to toss his cards away when Nell spoke up again.

"*He's very nervous, Gable.*" In his mind he answered the voice while he examined his cards,

"What are you talking about? He's a brick wall, strong hand for sure."

"*I sense he's very nervous,*" repeated the voice.

Reluctantly, Gable took his friend's advice and threw in the rest of his chips before laying down his hand. The salesman's expression changed immediately and he flicked his cards over in front of the dealer. He didn't even have a pair! He'd been bluffing the whole hand! Gable couldn't believe it when he had to take the pot back in front of him and the man left the table. The ladies chirped up as soon as the man had tossed his cards away.

"I knew you were a gambler!" said Maggie. "So that's how you do it girls," she said turning to the other pair. "You can't let them fool ya'!"

"I thought for sure he had you on that one," the other player chimed in off to his left. "How did you know you had him with the twos? What gave him away?"

"I guess I just had a hunch!" He actually didn't know what to say. Over the next half hour he seemed unable to be bluffed or led astray on the table. He was up roughly $1,200 and had gained himself quite a crowd. By now the old ladies had been given chairs to sit in and were fully engrossed in the game. Gable had even earned himself the attention of one of the floor bosses who had already comped him and the ladies a free lunch. It was blatantly obvious how having the ability to read one's mind could easily pay off in this town.

"You're doing remarkably well, sir," said the floor manager standing next to the attractive dealer. "You keep this up and we'll have to put you up on the Amateur's Wall of Fame!" That caught Gable's attention.

"Wall of Fame?" he questioned back.

"Something we used to do, sir. It was just a comment, please play on and enjoy yourself." He then quietly asked the dealer if she was all set and then backed away from the table.

Gable watched the man walk away into the field of tables. He fidgeted with his multiple stacks of chips and then quickly turned to Harriet who was sitting closest behind him.

"Ok, Harriet. It's up to you. I'll be right back." Her face beamed as she slid into Gable's chair and took his position at the table. The other ladies gave her quick words of encouragement and both began trying to whisper instructions to her. They had only ever seen the game played in the last hour and where excited to start with such an amount. Gable had squeezed through the small group of people and was scanning for the man who had mentioned that Wall of Fame. He spotted him standing against a wall not far away. He walked at a quick pace over to him.

"Good afternoon," Gable said as he approached with his hand extended. As they shook hands he continued, "My name is Gable Flagstaff. This is a great casino."

"Thank you, Mr. Flagstaff. You're doing very well today. Are you having fun?" Behind Gable a low sound came from the crowd at the table.

"Oh yeah, I'm having great beginner's luck over there. You mentioned something about an Amateur's Wall of Fame? Were you serious? Is there such a thing?"

"It was something the owners liked to do for the exceptional beginners. They stopped doing it years ago when they found out it didn't actually bring any profit in the door. It doesn't exist anymore. Why? Looking to get famous today?" he chuckled slightly as he leaned back against the wall.

"No, not me." Another quite murmur from his table forced him to turn back and look. There were a few more people now and he could just make out the three bright red hats in the center of it all. "When did they stop doing the Wall?" he persisted as he turned his head back towards the man.

"Years ago. You seem real interested. If you want to see it it's still in a storage room under a sheet somewhere in the back. I just saw it a few days ago. This place never throws anything out."

"That'd be great!" he said with enthusiasm.

"Sure, what do I care. C'mon it's this way." The floor manager walked a few feet down the wall and pushed through a door marked 'AUTHORIZED PERSONELL ONLY'. As Gable followed, he heard another loud shout from the crowd and leaned back to try to catch a glimpse.

"You coming?" said the man from the narrow service corridor. "It's back here." Gable promptly stepped into the corridor letting the door close behind him.

"Are you here Nell?" he said to himself.

"I am. Why are we interested in this 'Wall'?"

"Another hunch Nell. Maybe your friend made the Wall of Fame. He would have won a lot of money quick like we did." They came to a door on the left side of the hall as the manager pulled out a cluttered key chain from inside his vest and brought it to the doorknob

"This room's a wreck, brace yourself." He pulled the key back from the lock and swung it open with his left arm as he stepped inside. When he hit the lights Gable could see what the warning was all about. There was clutter everywhere. The floor in general was strewn with miscellaneous objects while in one corner there were damaged card tables stacked up with chairs loosely piled next to them. Against the far wall were two garment carts full of hanging employee uniforms in plastic covers. The other corner was fully occupied by what looked like a large board covered with a sheet. The man walked directly over to it and pulled away the dusty cloth exposing the words 'Amateur's Wall of Fame' in dull gold letters across the top. Both men waved off the floating dust in the air and stepped up to the display. It had six pictures across the middle with names and consecutive years below each snapshot. The first one was labeled 1994.

"Who's that guy?" Gable said while waving off the dust and pointing at the 1994 picture with his other hand.

"That guy? I wasn't here at the time but I guess that's the guy that convinced the owners to start this thing. That guy was a legend on his first day in the casino; they say he took away 50,000 dollars that day."

"His 'first' day?" Gable continued the conversation as he knelt down to the 8 by 10 picture of the man sitting behind stacks of chips.

"Yeah, I guess he bought a house and stuck around for a few years. Made a boat load of money before he blew out of town though. That was a long time ago."

"What's this name here under the picture?" Gable leaned forward wiping off grime from the plaque.

"*THAT'S THE CLERIC!!!!!*" shouted Nell in Gable's head. He could feel Nell was directly behind him.

Chapter 21

At the observatory, the inspection had been in full swing all morning. The lead contractor was touring around Mr. Neil Allen and he wanted to see everything that belonged to his program.

"As always, it's good to have you down Neil," said the contractor as they strolled across the ground where eventually 350 radio dishes would be positioned. The empty spaces had all been marked out and conduit sprouting wire was coming from the ground in the center most of them. They spent at least an hour standing at the first large completed dish while operators inside the building took it through its paces. Neil wanted to see that every movement was smooth and precise.

"When complete how soon could the array of dishes focus on a single point if a signal is received from deep space?" he quizzed the builder.

"Once built all dishes will home on a signal within seconds. If someone's trying to talk to us out there, your array will find it. We really appreciate your efforts on this project, Neil. It's good to see private investors such as yourself take such an interest," said the contractor standing next to the dish. Neil was up on a side step of the large unit and hopped down onto the dusty soil.

"It's a passion really. Now you say you've got five more dishes on site ready for installation?"

"Yes. Units two through six are in the storage hanger across the grounds there." He pointed in the distance to an opened door hanger at least two hundred yards away.

"If you don't mind I'd like to check those units out before lunch." He turned to the contractor with a commanding stare.

"Uhm, sure," the man seemed to stutter out the answer. "I'm going to go in and check on our lunch orders. Knowing you, I guess I'll meet you inside in about forty minutes?"

"Yeah, sounds good," Neil answered as he began to walk towards the hanger. He was excited to see the progress on the project and was eager to inspect the five new radio dishes. He quickly made his way to the doorway of the hangar where the large sliding doors were wide open shedding good light all the way to the back of the crowded hangar. Most everything was covered in heavy gray tarps and unmarked. He was immediately disgusted with the disorganization. Near the back was a large tarp that seemed newer that the others in the building and it caught his eye. He made his way to the back of the hanger stepping on corners of pallets and tripping over loose equipment that almost seemed like it was intentionally put in the way. When he got to the clear area around the large tarped object he could see the massive wheeled dolly protruding out from the bottom.

"Must be big," he thought. He flipped back a corner of the tarp revealing the smooth contour and light coloring of the alien craft in hiding! Neil gasped and staggered back from the exposed shell in disbelief. He took a few seconds to collect himself and then stepped back towards the strange sight with an outreached hand. As he touched the smooth outer surface of the craft he instantly disappeared.

Meanwhile Dr. Richards was busy giving his empty presentation to Senator Brandt and guests in a small boardroom in the office area of the disguised silo. The Senator had brought with him four other staunchly dressed businessmen who were very tight lipped and nervous to be there. Senator Brandt did most of the talking and the others only seemed to chime into the presentation only when there where obvious discrepancies or mistakes in the information.

"Ed, you promised me proof for continued funding. I don't see that here! It boils down to one specimen you've got in a tank, a busted spacecraft that's so deteriorated it's barely recognizable and another one that you can't get inside of! The tangible results from the first alien have yielded almost nothing, and that creature from what I understand is on its last leg!"

"That's not true, Senator," retorted the doctor. "We've been able to transport many test subjects and even completed human trials."

"Is it not true that your process needs to have a decompression chamber at the delivery point?! And what about the memory loss side effects I'm reading about in this report?!" He pulled from a briefcase a report that Dr. Richards had written after they pulled dozens of homeless people through the chamber. "What is our candidate supposed to say in the debates; that he'll bring your boys home, but sorry, they won't know who the hell they are!"

"That's precisely why I need continued funding, Senator. This Gable Flagstaff might hold the key to the next round of research. I believe that he has been passed on this transport ability by one of the creatures at the 2004 landing."

"But listen, Doctor, you have no creatures to compare between landings, you have no proof that this man is nothing more than a civilian, and you haven't been able to get inside this new ship to prove that it's even the same technology. You could be starting over from scratch here and I don't think we're totally convinced to ride this out again. We needed results now with enough time before the '08 election to establish our man." The room was tense. Senator Brandt had remained seated as he voiced his argument, while Dr. Richards had been up and down from his chair defending his research aggressively. He had a small sweat forming and was very happy to see the secretary bringing in lunch. The subs and sodas would keep the guests occupied for a bit while Richards excused himself.

"If you'll excuse me, gentlemen, I have a phone call I need to make. I won't be long." He left the room as the others began opening the tray of food. Dr. Richards took a fast paced walk down the hall to his office and burst through the door. Within moments Captain Mitchell's cell phone was vibrating in his pocket. He pulled it out and recognized the number.

"I'm close, doc. I'm in Reno right now and my men will rendezvous within the hour. Just relax," he quickly said.

"RELAX? Need I remind you that we are trying to secure our careers here? I have bunk here to go on! I'm about to show them a rotting alien and a tin can I can't open. Where is Gable Flagstaff?!?"

"I'm on the streets now. We'll case the casinos when my men arrive. That's the best I can do. OUT." He quickly snapped the phone shut, and slid it back in the chest pocket of his fatigues. He was cruising the main streets now keeping a sharp eye out for his target.

Chapter 22

"Neil Allen?" Gable said as he squinted at the faded plaque.

"Yep, that's him. They say he was the luckiest player anyone's ever seen. If I had his streaks I would have retired in this town. I guess he had better things to do. So anyways, this is the Wall of Fame I was talking about, but I've gotta get you back to the floor before I get in trouble. I've only been in this position for under a year so they probably wouldn't lose any sleep firing my ass." He threw the sheet back over the display and motioned for Gable to head to the door. Gable stood up and headed out to the narrow hall.

"Hey thanks for showing me the Wall, that's pretty neat stuff. I'll get back to my game and see if I can get on the Pro Wall!" he said jokingly as they walked.

"Ok sir, good luck out there!" He opened the door back onto the casino floor and turned left away from the tables, leaving Gable standing by the wall.

"We have a name, Nell!" he whispered.

"*A name will speed our search then?*" the ghost answered.

"Oh yeah. He lived here for years too! We could find his old house, get a forwarding address, look him up on the web, ...we've got him now Nell!" He could barely contain his excitement!

He started to venture towards the table he had left only ten minutes ago, and quickly noticed something was wrong. The table was empty and a new dealer was now manning the station.

"Where did everybody go?" Gable asked.

"Everybody, sir?" the dealer asked quietly as he leaned over the table.

"Where did the old ladies go? Where'd the money go?" His questions faded as he stepped back from the table and caught a glimpse of the tips of three red hats peeking over the slot machines in the distance. He strode across the maze of tables and machines until he came around the corner by the three ladies viciously feeding the slots. They saw him immediately.

"There you are!" Maggie chirped. "Now before you get mad at us, we have to tell you that we lost all your chips. That game is much harder than we thought." The other two nodded in agreement as they sat clutching their plastic buckets full of quarters.

"That's ok ladies. Listen, I found my friend so I'll be taking off now. It was great meeting you though." He extended his hand and Maggie slid off her chair and right into a hug.

"Now you take care, Sweetie," she said as she squeezed him. The other two offered similar good byes before he was actually allowed to leave their sight.

He quickly headed out of the casino and back into the sunshine of the street.

"Ok, Nell, we've gotta find a clerk's office or a municipal building, let's start looking!" He turned right, which was just as good a choice as any, and headed down the sidewalk.

"*You are very energized, Gable,*" said Nell as he tried to keep pace.

"This is our big break! We should be able to find this Cleric with little problem now!"

Chapter 23

Neil Allen, familiar with the ship's design, had teleported himself inside. He was jubilant to be aboard. He hadn't seen any sign of his planet in twelve years and now he couldn't believe it. He hustled over to an outcrop on the bright wall and placed his hand on a red oval shape on the surface. He stood for a moment before his eyes glossed over and his mind began to meld with the ship. The ship's system's acted as an amplifier as it sent a powerful strand of cerebral energy blasting to a point 12 billion light years away. A loud voice seemed to boom through the room, but it was all in the Cleric's head.

"Cleric?" came a voice back from deep space. "We had feared the worse. Where is your escort?"

"I know of no 'escort'. I am alone, but I believe I can pilot this ship back now," he voiced back impatiently.

"There has been enough interaction with the human kind; find the escort and return immediately. We cannot risk you piloting the ship alone; to lose you now would be detrimental. We have reported to the Nell that your spiritual journey has gone well but that you were returning soon. The members of the High Clergy will welcome your return." The voice seemed Godly in its tone and the Cleric even after years of isolation on Earth knew to obey. "We have received reports frequently from the escort, remain with the ship until he returns."

"I will wait for his return and then we will begin our journey very shortly. I do so miss our world and am eager to return. That's all." When the transmission ended it sent a shock through his body that would have snapped a human's neck. His eyes then slowly cleared as he shook his stare from the wall and his hand slid from the control. He took a few hard steps back from the console and looked around the ship. It was only a matter of time now before he would return to his home and he was filled with happiness as he stared at the bright walls and ceiling.

Meanwhile Gable and his invisible companion were strolling down the sidewalks of Reno with the world by the tail. The mystery of the Cleric and his identity had been broken. Finding someone with a name is far easier than searching for a face among the millions.

"*I think I will return to the ship for nutrition now,*" said Nell.

"You're right pal, it is dinner time. I was so excited about the break in the case I'd forgotten to eat too!" He pulled out his ticket for the complimentary lunch that the casino had given him and wished he'd thought of that before he ran out of there. He looked about and spotted a fast food restaurant and decided to get a bite to eat himself. He stopped only feet from the restaurant door and to passerby's he seemed to have a few words with himself.

"Hey look Nell, let's not be so long this time, ok?" He still got a little shaky when he thought about the rollover on the highway.

"*Minimal time, and then I'll return here.*"

"Greatly appreciated. See you in 10 minutes, all right? ... Nell?" No answer. "I hate when he does that." He shook his head with a grin and stepped forward to enter the restaurant.

"Stop right there Flagstaff!" hollered Captain Mitchell as he rounded the front of his parked car. He had spotted Gable walking the sidewalk and sneakily parked his car ahead of him. Gable froze in his tracks and then stepped back into a stiff standing position continuing to face away from the voice. The Captain stepped onto the sidewalk roughly fifteen feet away and rested his hand on the butt of his holstered Tazer. Gable slowly turned around to face his suitor as pedestrians stopped on the sidewalk on both sides of the two men.

Nell instantly materialized visible on the deck of his immaculate ship to find the human form of Neil Allen standing near a floating holographic image. It seemed to be projected from the wall and was showing him images, like a television, of scenes from their home planet. Nell stood in awe! Here was the Cleric, on his ship, standing idle waiting to return home after a year of searching for even clues of his existence. He couldn't believe his eye!

"It's good of you to return. I am ready to go home now, let's begin." The Cleric waved off the screen and strode over to Nell.

"How did you get here? Where did you come from? We've been searching for you and now you just appear! This is amazing!"

"There are more of you? Splendid. Do you have a Braxton with you? I've missed their protection."

"My Braxton was destroyed when I landed. I have paired with a human to search for you. We were very close to finding you and now...now you have appeared. I must go back and get him. He will be pleased. He will now be freed from the scientists here."

"I have communicated with the High Clergy and they say to leave immediately. We are not to be involved with humans here any longer. I have grown tired of this race, although they are very easy to manipulate. It has taken me years, to finally develop an instrument here powerful enough to receive a signal from our planet, yet all the while the High Clergy has sent someone for me. Well I am here as well as you are, and we can leave. Shall we?" He swung his hand out as if to offer the ship to be piloted away. Nell sensed that the Cleric was going to be very forceful about leaving immediately. Back on his home planet, an adult Nell wouldn't think to disobey or ignore a High Clergy member, but they weren't home, and like Gable, Nell had gained a confidence that he thought he didn't have.

"I have given my word to this human. I must go back and retrieve him now." He stepped closer to the Cleric. *"The Clergy would not be happy to know you have left a Braxton alive and in the hands of the humans for the past twelve years."*

"My Braxton is alive?!" he shot back

"He is at a level of life, though not fully alive. They hold him in a building in a state of animation and have used him to explore our powers of teleportation. I'm SURE they're not going to be pleased with that." Nell had picked up a small sense of sarcasm from his time with Gable, and it seemed to take the Cleric by surprise. He continued his proposal as he stepped in further to the humanoid.

"Are you one of those Clerics who's meddled with your genetic makeup enough to lose your invisibility? If you aren't, you can use my memory of the building to clean up your own mess, I'll be going after my friend." He now stood within arms reach of the alien in human form.

"Very well, escort." Neil Allen put his hand on Nell's shoulder and absorbed from him the memory he had of the inside of the silo. He finished the absorption of Nell's memory, arduously became invisible and then transported himself out of the ship.

Chapter 24

"You're a tough guy to find Gable." Captain Mitchell stated as he sidestepped near the side of his car. Gable kept his distance and softly stepped in the opposite direction. The sight of a military officer in the middle of the day bearing down on a plainclothes civilian had drawn obvious attention. Captain Mitchell left his hand on the holstered weapon and addressed the forming crowd with a loud voice.

"This man is a violent criminal and a fugitive from the military. Please everyone stay back," he said as he motioned with his free hand for the people to stay away. He then turned his attention back to Gable and continued in a lower tone.

"I know your secret, I know how you've been jumping around. You've got their ability now. Well, we'll never let you go now, Gable. You've got nowhere to go anyway. We've burned your house to the ground and your brother is going to have a short recovery when he wakes up if you don't come with me right now." Mitchell took a half step towards Gable as he fidgeted nervously on the sidewalk.

"Well, maybe I'll just transport out now!" he threatened and he started to ease away from the soldier. The Captain quickly drew out his yellow tipped Tazer and cast a laser dot onto Gable's chest.

"I don't think you're going anywhere but with me!" The crowd flinched at the action, but Gable merely looked down at the dot. As he brought his eyes back up to face the gunman, he continued his bluff.

"If I was to transport away, where would you look then? I could disappear forever."

"I have a theory, don't you worry. So let's just make this easy, huh." He held the targeting dot firm on his chest and took one step forward. Gable held eye contact for only a second and then threw himself onto the sidewalk. Captain Mitchell pulled the trigger full on his weapon and the yellow air capsule pack on the tip of the gun ejected the two electrodes out against the restaurant window front, missing Gable by inches as he dropped. He scrambled on the sidewalk to get up and run, but Captain Mitchell pulled the failed tip off the end of his Tazer and reloaded with the spare air capsule from the butt of his gun with a fluid motion. His second shot was an easier one as Gable scrambled to his feet and exposed his back to the steady targeting laser.

The prongs from the electrodes dug in and carried the stiffening current down the wires from the end of the gun. It would deliver five seconds of paralyzing voltage as the gun clicked away; it would be a long five seconds for Gable. His body immediately went stiff as he fell forward like a board on the pavement. His arms crossed tight across his chest as he took the shocks.

Captain Mitchell let him take the full duration from the Tazer and then walked forward to kneel next to Gable on the sidewalk. The effects of the Tazer left him as soon as the time was up, but Gable had landed on his arm and hit his head during the fall. He now groaned in pain as the wires draped from his back to the gun in the hands of the man next to him.

"What's wrong? Your abilities need a little reenergizing? Hmm?" he said mockingly. "You're coming with me now, let's go." He stood up still holding the weapon, ready to pull the trigger again if Gable didn't follow. "Let's go!" he shouted down to him.

Suddenly Gable disappeared! The electrodes and length of spooled out wire fell to the empty pavement. The crowd gasped as the body disappeared before their eyes.

"Bastard!" The gun dropped from Captain Mitchell's hand as he frantically grabbed at his pocket for his phone. He'd put the technician in the Chamber Room on speed dial and called him quickly to put his back-up plan in affect. Depending on the Doctor's theory, he figured Gable had transported himself back to the observatory and the ship. When the technician activated the chamber, he would be able to transport back and cut him off. The technician answered the call.

"Now dammit, now!" the Captain barked into the phone.

"Receiving your phone's location now sir," said the technician.

The alien known as Neil Allen had teleported himself inside the hidden facility according to Nell's visions and made his way undetected to the room below, where the Braxton's suspended body lay entombed in the stainless steel case. He stood there amongst the bustling technicians and activity of the room staring down through the glass at the body deteriorating in the fluid of the case. A loud hum came from the ceiling and the room above as the Chamber Room emitted deep vibrations. The Braxton began to flinch in the fluid, as the powerful computers in the Chamber Room above demanded the power from its mind. No one detected Neil as he calmly rested his invisible hands on the lid of the case.

"Rest now my Braxton. Let me control." As his words faded, the Cleric fell into a heavy trance as the Braxton slumped inside. Up one floor an observer slid open the round viewing hatch on the decompression chamber to see a dazed and confused Captain Mitchell looking around in the dark. Suddenly he was gone! The observer spun quickly and alerted the technician.

"We've lost him! There's a disruption in the transport, he's disappeared from the chamber!" Somewhere high above Yellowstone Park in the flight path of his crash landing years ago, Neil had transported the confused Captain. He instantly appeared hundreds of feet above the forest floor and immediately began his fatal descent. The effects of the machine transportation left him with no recollection of why he was falling or why he was there. He just knew there was empty space and the rushing sound of wind all around him. The scream was only audible for a few seconds and then the silence of the park once again took over.

People were scattering all over the Chamber Room and frantically running systems checks on all the computers as Neil slowly recovered from his trance. He slowly removed his hands from the case and looked deep into the glass. He had no thoughts as he reached below the case and unlatched the two-inch tube that cycled the fluid through the coffin.

Suddenly fluid was rushing quickly out the large opening and dumping all over the floor under the alien's case. It only took seconds for the tank to drain and as the Cleric watched the fluid level drop through the glass, every part of the Braxton that exposed itself immediately disintegrated and dissolved into the solution. Technicians and computer analysts scrambled over to the scene as the Cleric quietly moved to the far side of the room so that the rushing people wouldn't discover him. He thought the chaos was almost comical.

"What the hell happened?!" yelled the room manager. "Reconnect that pipeline!" he ordered to his people, but it was too late. By the time someone had picked up the large diameter line from the floor only long strands and drips of fluid seeped from the drain hole of the tank.

"Someone get me Richards!" he forcibly asked as he stood in disbelief by the tank. He looked down into the tank at the pools of fluid trapped in the corners and the wires and the tangled hookups. Everything was lying peacefully on the bottom of the empty tank.

In the office area Dr. Richards had been struggling to keep the attention of the Senator and his partners. The presentation had not been going well since the day began, and it was about to go far worse.

"Dr. Richards?" the speaker in the center of the conference table asked.

"Excuse me gentlemen," Dr. Richards said as he walked back from the white board at the front of the room. He pressed the 'TALK' button on the unit and acknowledged the secretary.

"Dr. Richards, I have an urgent call for you. Would you like to take it on a different phone?" He looked about the room at his guests and could see they were already irritated by the interruption.

"No, I'll take it here, patch it through." Suddenly the speaker erupted with the sounds of commotion.

"Dr. Richards! There's been an accident in here! We've lost the alien! Something happened with the tank! You've got to get in here!" In the background there were sounds of disorder and people rushing about.

Senator Brandt and the other men now sat forward nervously in their chairs listening to the frazzled technician.

"I'll be right there! Stabilize the situation man!" He slammed another button, terminating the call, and then pushed back from the large table. The Senator spoke up first.

"If you think that we're not going with you, you're seriously mistaken." He rose quickly and faced his partners. "It sounds to me gentlemen that our investment is falling apart even quicker that we thought." He stood staring across the table at the Doctor.

"Well then let's go," he lamented as he dashed from the conference table and burst out into the office area. The entourage followed close behind as he walked at a brisk pace away from the offices. Within moments he erupted through the doorway into the room below the Chamber. He couldn't believe the scene! A technician in a lab coat was actually mopping the floor below the tank and another was pacing back and forth punching the keys on his hand held computer tablet. The room manager sat in a chair only a few feet away with his head propped up in the palms of his hands in an obvious daze.

"What happened here?!" The Doctor stepped out onto the wet tiled floor as the Senator and the others filed in behind him. He slowly panned over to the man sitting in the chair, who answered in a monotone voice.

"I don't know...one moment we were transporting Captain Mitchell and the next the tank began to suddenly drain and the Chamber Room reported that we had lost him in transmission. Now the tank is empty and the creature dissolved when the fluid left. I don't know what the hell happened!"

"Captain Mitchell was using the transporter?! What do you mean you lost him?!" He spoke as he walked up to the dripping case in the center of the room. He rested his hands on the edges and looked down through the glass.

"We had him in the chamber for only a second and then he was gone again. There's no way to trace him now." The man rose from the chair and stepped over to the tank next to Dr. Richards who was holding a blank stare down into the empty box.

"How did this tank drain out?" he asked quietly to the man in disbelief.

"We have no idea, sir. The feed line just came apart. It evacuated before we could reattach it." The Senator and his men were lightly fanning out from the doorway stepping on all the dry tiles they could find. The Senator himself accidentally stepped in a large puddle of pooling fluid next to the tank. He pulled his foot from the floor and watched the ooze strand off the soul.

"So this is what you're spending our money on, Doctor?" Richards hadn't looked up from the box yet and to him it felt as if the room was spinning. He didn't have Gable to prove out his research and with the Captain missing, he was sure he was never going to get him. The old ship from the crash had been falling to pieces since they brought it back, and the other ship was seemingly impenetrable. And now below him, the engine to his transportation machine had just gone down the drain.

Chapter 25

Under the tarp in the hangar Nell had transported Gable from the sidewalk in Reno. Gable lie on the pristine floor of the spacecraft, trying to hold his head and arm at the same time while Nell sat quietly next to him.

"Ugh," he muttered, "Ok, new rule, we're not separating again." He rolled to his back and covered his eyes with his hands while he adjusted to the bright interior.

"*I bring good news, Gable. Our search is over.*" The figure of Neil Allen stepped over from behind the crouched alien. The Cleric had gone back to the ship moments after the frantic men had called for Richards. He arrived just moments after Nell. Gable squinted as he looked up at the man.

"Where did you come from?" he questioned. The Cleric did not answer the question, rather he asked Nell one of his own.

"So this is your human friend?" Nell spoke up quickly.

"*Gable I'd like you to meet the Cleric, the one we've been searching for.*" Gable sat up as his eyes had now fully adjusted to the light. He looked over the man and instantly recognized him from the picture on the Wall of Fame at the casino. He hadn't appeared to age a bit. Neil Allen returned the stare and seemed to read his thoughts.

"If you are concerned with a Captain Mitchell, you can put your mind at ease. He won't be bothering you anymore," he gloated to the human. Gable picked himself off the floor as Nell rose with him. He trusted the words from the strange man without question, but was still concerned about the persistence of Dr. Richards. His mind was an open book to both aliens who stood before him.

"When we leave in this ship, friend, he will have no cause to pursue you. He will be ruined. This ship is the last piece of standing evidence that we were ever here. You're brother should awaken from the drug soon and you will be free."

"This is unbelievable," he muttered. "I've been hiding from all this for a year and now it's almost over." He was looking about the ship for he knew it was close to the last time he would ever see it, and then he panned to Neil standing close to his new friend. "You've been hiding pretty well for a long time, I can't say I'm sad to see you found."

"I've barely been hiding, Mr. Flagstaff. In fact my every effort since the crash has been to contact my kind. Over the years I've gained enough wealth to have the humans begin to build the largest extraterrestrial listening device that's ever been conceived. In one more year's time, I would have been able to receive a signal from our planet light years away. Without my ship to enhance my mental ability it was impossible for me to send a signal back, but I thought if I left a marker here on the planet that someday a rescue attempt would be able to easily find me." He shot Nell a disappointed glance as he waved his hand in front of him summoning the translucent screen to appear between himself and Gable. With a finger the alien began to write on the surface. It was as if he was drawing on a steamy mirror that Gable could see through with all the letters in reverse. Neil Allen was writing his name on the surface of the screen as Gable interpreted from the other side. N E L L A L I E N. It hit him like a ton of bricks.

"Un-freaking-believable," he stated as he shot a look at Nell.

Meanwhile Dr. Richards had collected himself the best he could and had moved his ill-fated tour outside to the grounds. They were now crossing the dusty ground and heading for the hangar.

"I can show you gentlemen the new ship we've acquired. This I believe is of the same species of creature as the crash years ago. Once inside we'll be able to prove that theory and continue the research." The Senator and company struggled to keep up with the fast walking pace of the Doctor.

"Why is this thing out here, Richards? Why isn't it in a controlled environment? What sort of standards are you following!" he yelled forward at the trotting man. Without breaking stride he answered back over his shoulder,

"It became necessary to move the craft, Senator. I know what I'm doing." The fact was that he could see everything slipping away from him and he was losing control.

They briskly entered the hangar and stumbled back through all the equipment until reaching the large tarped craft. Inside the ship, the Cleric spun abruptly towards the far wall and waved off the screen. He quickly stepped over and pressed his palm against the wall. A large area of the bright wall faded to dark as it reveled the backside of the covering tarp draped on the exterior.

"This is the ship that will be the focus of our new research!" Richard reached down to the corner of the tarp and flipped it up. From inside the ship it appeared as if the occupants were looking out a triangular section of one-way glass at the gathering of men outside. The Cleric scowled at the men as he watched their mouths talk about the ship. Nell turned to Gable and calmly said,

"It's time to send you back now, friend. You've given me hope that your kind and mine could coexist peacefully and for all of it I thank you. I will present our journey to the High Clergy when we return and hopefully with time they will allow your planet to discover ours." Nell extended his

slender hand forward. Gable reached forward to accept the handshake and gripped it firmly.

"Thanks for saving my butt, and have a safe journey home," he said smiling at the emotionless face.

"*Farewell Gable Flagstaff.*" With a final squeeze of his hands, Gable disappeared from the ship. The Cleric's hand left the wall as he strode over to his escort; the bright wall filling in behind him.

"Let's leave now. We've interfered enough!" He was highly bothered by the men outside the nose of the ship and wanted nothing more than to be on their way for the long journey.

"*As you wish Cleric.*" Nell stepped over to the outcrop on the wall with the red shaded button and held his right hand a few inches above it. He put his left hand on top of his other and then lowered himself to his knees in front of the control without touching the button. He concentrated hard for a moment and then slipped into a trance.

Outside the ship, Doctor Richards was arguing with the Senator about all the failed attempts to crack the shell of the exterior and gain access.

"There are still things yet to try, Senator! All I need is a little more time and funding to bring me to the next year. Surely with this ship and my proposed tests with Gable Flagstaff it's enough to convince you?"

Nell's body fully slipped into the trance as his mind melded with the ships circuitry. His hands fell limp on the large red shape and the ship instantly disappeared!

Behind Richards the air escaped from beneath the tarp and it slowly slumped to the ground. The four business partners with the Senator jumped back against some loose equipment and stumbled into the pallets on the floor. Richards spun as the air pushed past him and the tarp settled flat in the large open space on the hangar floor. The ship was gone! He stood in disbelief, speechless.

Senator Brandt stepped close behind the frozen man and spoke only a few words.

"This research is over Richards. You will not pursue this Flagstaff person and you'll clean this mess up. If I ever hear from you again or see your name and 'alien' in the same sentence, you'll lose more than your reputation." Dr. Richards remained still as he took in the information. He was focusing more on just trying to stand. The Senator turned and stormed past the other men who were stumbling over the junk in the area.

"Let's go gentlemen, we were never here!" He walked from the hangar with his following, leaving Dr. Richards in the distance staring down at his empty tarp.

Chapter 26

Gable found himself standing in front of the same glass pane he had been at the day before; in the visiting room of the ICU. A nurse walked into the room and was startled by Gable standing there blankly looking through he glass.

"Sir? She said from the doorway. "He's awake if you'd like to go see him. I believe he's just resting, go ahead," she said persuading him. Gable was trying to absorb everything that had happened to him in the past days and months. It was all over, he was safe now and it was hard to grasp in an instant. He looked over to the nurse and stepped towards the door.

"Thank you!" he exclaimed to her as he gave her a big hug.

"Oh, you're welcome," she said surprisingly. He released her and moved into the room where his brother was peacefully resting. He stood next to the bed holding onto the bedrail as he tried to control his emotion. Jake stirred a little and then opened his eyes.

"Hey bro," he said sleepily as his eyes tried to focus.

"Hey Jake, how you feeling?"

"Good, I guess. They say a car hit me? I don't remember a thing, I guess I must have been hit good then." He dragged himself up in the angled bed and looked over the side at Gable's foot.

"Hey man, you've got a hole in your shoe." They both peered down at the perfect half-inch hole in Gable's left shoe to see his white sock inside. "How'd you do that?"

"It's a long story, Jake, maybe someday I'll tell you all about it."